COME WITH THE WIND

NICODEMUS

TELLS HIS STORY

A BIOGRAPHICAL NOVEL

BY

DONALD V GOODRIDGE

WITH FOREWORD BY

GENERAL BRAMWELL TILLSLEY

EPHESIANS 3:19.

Other books written by Donald V Goodridge

"The Family of God – From Religion to Divine Relationship"
Guardian Books – Published 2004

Note for Librarians: A cataloguing record for this book is available from Library
and Archives Canada at www.collectionscanada.ca/amicus/index-e.html

Printed in Victoria, BC, Canada.

ISBN: 978-1-4251-9233-4 (sc)
ISBN: 978-1-4251-9234-1 (hc)
ISBN: 978-1-4251-9235-8 (eBook)

*Our mission is to efficiently provide the world's finest, most comprehensive book publishing
service, enabling every author to experience success. To find out how to publish your
book, your way, and have it available worldwide, visit us online at www.trafford.com*

Trafford rev. 10/09/09

 **www.trafford.com**

North America & international
toll-free: 1 888 232 4444 (USA & Canada)
phone: 250 383 6864 ♦ fax: 812 355 4082

This book is dedicated to Elsie
My beloved wife of 53 years
The mother of our five children
My Sister in Christ
My partner in the Gospel
Without whose encouragement
And practical assistance
This book could not have been written

THE GOSPEL OF JOHN

3: 1 – 21

Now there was a man of the Pharisees named Nicodemus, a member of the Jewish ruling council. He came to Jesus at night and said, "Rabbi, we know you are a teacher who has come from God. For no one could perform the miraculous signs you are doing if God were not with him."

In reply Jesus declared, "I tell you the truth, no one can see the kingdom of God unless he is born again."

"How can a man be born when he is old?" Nicodemus asked. "Surely he cannot enter a second time into his mother's womb to be born!"

Jesus answered, "I tell you the truth, no one can enter the kingdom of God unless he is born of water and the Spirit. Flesh gives birth to flesh, but the Spirit gives birth to spirit. You should not be surprised at my saying, 'You must be born again.' The wind blows wherever it pleases. You hear the sound, but you cannot tell where it comes from or where it is going. So it is with everyone born of the Spirit."

"How can this be?" Nicodemus asked.

"You are Israel's teacher," said Jesus, "and do you not understand these things? I tell you the truth, we speak of what we know, and we testify to what we have seen, but still you people do not accept our testimony. I have spoken to you of earthly things and you do not believe; how then will you believe if I speak of heavenly things? No one has ever gone into heaven except the one who came from heaven – the Son of Man. Just as Moses lifted up the snake in the desert, so the Son of Man must be lifted up, that everyone who believes in him may have eternal life.

"For God so loved the world that he gave his one and only Son, that whoever believes in him shall not perish but have eternal life. For God did not send his Son into the world to condemn the world, but to save the world through him. Whoever believes in him is not condemned, but whoever does not believe stands condemned already because he has not believed in the name of God's one and only Son. This is the verdict: Light has come into the world, but men loved darkness instead of light because their deeds were evil. Everyone who does evil hates the light, and will not come into the light for fear that his deeds will be exposed. But whoever lives by the truth comes into the light, so that it may be seen plainly that what he has done has been done through God."

(New International Version)

Table of Contents

Foreword

DONALD GOODRIDGE HAS provided us with a carefully researched biographical novel of Nicodemus, a Pharisee and ruler of the Jews. The novel is based on the visit of Nicodemus with Jesus, recorded in chapter 3 of John's Gospel.

The author's purpose in writing was to "bring to the reader the spiritual and historic significance of an epic event of eternal consequence, leading to a full commitment to Jesus Christ."

One of the great challenges in such a work is to maintain an element of surprise, when many of the readers will be familiar with the story as recorded in John's Gospel. This has been accomplished by employing some creative imagination in places where the Scriptural account is silent. Throughout the novel the author has been true to the Biblical record.

To add to the element of surprise, the author makes good use of many of the minor characters of the drama including the wife of Nicodemus. A most interesting link is made throughout between Nicodemus and Joseph of Arimathea.

The reader will benefit greatly by the explanation of many Jewish terms and customs.

The novel is not a sermon but draws us personally into the account. We share in many of the decisions Nicodemus had to make.

The final chapter, "My Confession" is the personal experience of the author, and may not represent the individual experience of the reader. "The WIND blows this way and that. You hear it rustling through the trees, but you have no idea where it comes from and where it's headed next. That's the way it is with everyone born from above by the wind of God, the Spirit of God." (John 3:8; The Message)

"Come With The Wind" explains not only what is recorded in John's Gospel but also what is left out. The author possesses the rare gift of "sanctified imagination." Certainly you will be guided to new trends of thought as you move through the novel. The author has provided us with fresh inspiration as we contemplate not only God's leading in the life of Nicodemus, but also God's leading in our own lives as we are open to "the WIND of the Spirit."

Bramwell Tillsley
General

5/4/2009

Acknowledgements

The publishing of a book is never just the end result of the writing. There are many people, who directly and indirectly, contribute to its completion and release.

There are many readers of my first book who have enquired about and encouraged the writing of this one. I thank you all for your assurance that this offering will be appreciated.

I acknowledge the posting of multiple resources on the Internet from which I have drawn copiously, including:

Bryan T. Huie – Subject: The Jewish Sanhedrin, Mar. 16, 1997, Revised Sep. 19, 2008.

Jewish Encyclopedia.com – Subject: The Jewish Sanhedrin.

Wikipedia: The Free Encyclopedia – Making Life Easier – Subject: John The Apostle

Sayings of the Cross

Descent of The Holy Spirit

Chapel Perilous Copyright 1998 By Hague Productions – Subject: Mary Magdalene & Jesus.

Profiles of Joseph, Caiaphas and Pontius Pilate – Subject: The Trial of Jesus: Key Figures.

Meridian Gospel Doctrine – Who Was Nicodemus? by John A Tvedtnes.

Crucifixion – All About Jesus Christ – Subject: Crucifixion of Jesus.

All About Jesus Christ.org – Copyright 2002 – 2008 – (Diocesepb.org) – Subject: The Stations of the Cross.

Facing The Challenge Training Course – Subject: Simon of Cyrene.

Got Questions.org – Subject: Significance of the Temple.

To the best of my knowledge, I have not quoted verbatim from any of the above resources. I have incorporated materials into my storyline such as I deemed essential to the plot. Thank you all for your diligence and dedication in the support of the cause of Jesus Christ. I trust my efforts will speed your mission on its way.

I acknowledge the prayer support for this project that has been assured by everyone who has learned of this undertaking. It is humbling to experience the inspiration and discipline that begins in the prayer closet. I pray the results will confirm that your prayers have been answered.

My very special thanks go to my former pastors, Majors Les and Cathy Burrows, and my church family of the Kelowna Community Church of The Salvation Army. Their prayers I have always felt around me in my daily walk with God, but their interest in the writing of this book has added immeasurable depth to the prayer support, and much encouragement to its writing. God bless you all.

Of special significance is the tireless and meticulous proofing that my wife contributed to the book. "Elsie, only you could give such uncompromising critique to my writing, without damage to my ego. I love you for your integrity, and your sensitivity. Thank you!"

I acknowledge the uncompromising direction and encouragement of the publisher, Trafford Publishing. Your leap of faith in the accepting of this work greatly confirms the hand of God upon it that it should be written to his glory and the spiritual blessing of its readers.

Last but foremost, with gratitude well beyond words sufficient to express it, I acknowledge my thanks to General Bramwell Tillsley, 14th General and World Leader of The Salvation Army (1993 -1994), himself the author of four books, for his valuable advice and the writing of the Foreword for the book. God bless you Sir!

Preface

WHAT A JOURNEY it has been! In these pages you have the
second book I have been privileged to write.

It is however my first novel!

Though at first reluctant to write a second book, I confess to
the persistent prompting of the Holy Spirit that I should write a
book on this particular theme.

Through the deep sense of the Spirit's presence in my morning
devotional periods, I gained confirmation that I must put it off
no longer.

The story of Nicodemus needs to be told!

Those precious times in prayer and in the study of the Word
brought untold blessing to my labors.

Though his involvement in the biblical narrative is very scarce,
he is central with Jesus Christ in a major chapter in the Gospel of
John that has become pivotal to Christian faith and practice.

In my research I found that he holds significant influence beyond
the pages of our Protestant versions of the Holy Scriptures.

I have borrowed heavily from those additional sources, taking
great care to be true to our traditional scriptures that I hold to be
the divinely inspired word of God.

I do not quote frequently from the Bible, but my references
to those passages pertinent to the story line reflect accurately the
facts as they are disclosed in both the Old and New Testaments.

I concede to considerable poetic license in the building of
the plot, but nowhere that I am aware of do I contradict the
commonly held interpretations of scripture.

The sole objective of this book is to inspire you, the reader, to an uncompromising commitment to Jesus Christ and the truths of the Gospel Message.

I pray most sincerely that you will be truly uplifted in your faith journey, to the praise and glory of Jesus Christ, my Lord and Savior.

CHAPTER 1

"Hello"

IT WAS A dark and stormy night! No, this is not a spooky story around the camp fire, despite that I begin its writing on what used to be called "All Hallows Night," a celebration of the lives of Christian Saints, long since dead, though still alive (I'll explain later); and is now, in your time, called "Halloween."

This I assure you, it was a very dark and blustery night, with eerie, howling winds.

It was also a night of intrigue, one might say truthfully, a clandestine night that took place more than 2000 years ago.

I could never have guessed that it would lead to the exposure of what I believe to be the most diabolical plot against innocent human life ever recorded.

I concede that history has uncovered myriad unspeakable atrocities enacted by man against his fellowmen. But my story exposes a willful and savage attack by human kind against the very God of creation, all in the name of religion. In fact, it reveals the end result of power corrupted by high authority in achievement of personal gain, resulting in the incredulity of all spiritual pursuit.

Nor could I have ever imagined that my involvement in the story would literally put my life on the line, and would require of me decisions that would be life-changing, and would shake my belief system to the very core.

Oh, please forgive me! I have not introduced myself. My name is Nicodemus. Yes the very Nicodemus you can read about in the Gospel of John in the New Testament of the Holy Bible. How did John come to write about me in the first place? Well, its because he is actually involved in my story.

The three other writers of the Gospels do not mention this part of my story because they knew nothing of that night, and John's part in it.

The Apostle Peter, as it turned out, did have knowledge of the account I am about to give. He was the assumed leader of the twelve disciples, and generally was in on everything that concerned his Lord.

What came to pass that night was kept hush-hush because other human lives, not to mention mine, depended upon it. Indeed, the whole story was not revealed until John wrote his wonderful gospel that bears his name. Even then, only essential information was given.

It was an experience that in the beginning I would have never chosen for myself. It dramatically changed my life forever!

It was a night that left the destiny of my nation hanging in the balance and, as it turned out, the moment of truth for all mankind throughout all ages.

"Why me Lord?" Or, "O my God!" Either expletive has likely crossed our lips on more than one occasion. Seldom, if ever, is an individual faced with a decision that has life-or-death consequences, much less one that has one's eternity hanging in the balance. Such occasions never come with fanfare. Rarely do other people notice, not even loved ones. Yet, I found myself confronted with just such a decision: unavoidable, and exceedingly consequential.

As it turned out, that night would produce the greatest question ever to face mankind, and it would set in motion the greatest injustice the world would ever see again.

I do not suggest that other atrocities before or after this event do not match or even exceed the extremes of human suffering this story portrays. But I am talking about pitting human rebellion against divine purpose, producing a struggle that would sweep the generations of all peoples of the world, then and now, to the edge of eternity and the very brink of Hell.

Would I wish it never to have happened? Oh yes indeed! Was I ever glad for the outcome? Oh yes! Yes! Yes! A thousand times yes! But it is best that I delay the details so that you might better understand and perhaps empathize with my dilemma!

I am certain that you too will be caught up with the eternal consequences of the question posed!

"...Who do you say I am?"

(Matthew 16:15;)

CHAPTER 2

Credentials

Nicodemus, son of Gorion! "So?" I can understand your indifference. But as a Jew, other than Job of the Old Testament, my ancestry ranked among the highest in all Israel.

If personal wealth is held by some to be "the measure of the man," then I had it made. A wealth so exaggerated as to gossip that I could support all the inhabitants of Jerusalem for ten years.

But, "Son of Gorion" held far greater significance than the family fortune. The ancestry of a Jew was, and still is, of the greatest importance to the family influence among one's peers, with the most significant genealogies dating back to the days of Moses. In fact, the lineage of the person who is central to my story was traced back to Adam, the first human being to live on the earth, created by God himself.

He will take center-stage in the drama that will unfold within the pages of this book.

Not only was I a very rich man; of greater importance to me was my position as a Pharisee, afforded me by ancestral rite that can be traced back through the genealogies of the priesthood of our religion established by Aaron, brother to Moses. He was the first high priest of the Jewish religion.

Yes! I am a descendant of the tribe originally set apart by God from all the other tribes of Israel, for the practice and preservation of all religious observances associated with our nation - the tribe of Levi.

Could anyone have a greater inheritance? This far exceeded the influence of my wealth.

Yet strangely, both these blessings, wealth and religion, were to become the stumbling block to the preservation of my eternal soul.

There is a further source of influence that you need to know about as we proceed with my story.

I was a member of the Jewish Sanhedrin, the ruling government of the Jewish people, albeit under the dictatorial tyranny of our Roman conquerors.

Our Council was not a democratically elected body. There were seventy-two members, all appointed by the High Priest, albeit not without the consummate interest of the Roman Governor, Pilate.

The Sanhedrin comprised members of two opposing factions within our religion, the Pharisees and the Sadducees that, despite their ecclesiastical distinction, could pass as the government and opposition parties of modern day democracies.

The focal point of our differences was that we Pharisees believed in the resurrection of the dead. The Sadducees did not! This may not of itself give you any concern, but that doctrinal difference would prove to be the pivotal point of the drama that was soon to be enacted within this esteemed jurisdiction.

In all fairness, the Sadducees were originally a Jewish priestly order of deep spiritual significance within the life of our nation.

Over centuries of time they became entangled in godless religious dogmas that produced unbelief in any spiritual claims to a life hereafter, quickly eroding any thought of the need of a spiritual epiphany.

This meant that they shared no interest in the so-called "Messiah" we Pharisees had anticipated over the centuries of multiple enemy occupations and disbursements of our nation.

As for us Pharisees, we had always hoped for a spiritual deliverance and restoration to the fellowship of God through the promised Messiah. But such an aspiration had over time become reduced to the hope of national deliverance from our many enemies, especially the Romans who now occupied our land.

We were nonetheless considered to be the guardians of the Jewish Religion and as such wielded much influence within the Jewish community, although it is to the shame of our pharisaical hypocrisy that we no longer considered our estate to be in need of any "spiritual" reform whatsoever.

This meant that the influence of the Sadducees was now strictly political, voiding them of any conscience in whatever steps were needed to keep them in power.

This would greatly enhance the dangers I faced in any involvement with anyone that might be conceived as a threat to their illustrious status.

With nothing to lose from their perspective, and the entanglements of us Pharisees in our consummate preoccupation with Jesus of Nazareth, gave to the Sadducees every opportunity to compromise the integrity of any Pharisee they could point the finger at. What matter if one or more should die for the cause!

It is strange to me now, in reflection, how religious and political factions continuously assume such egotism as to justify the most hideous of crimes for the protection and advancement of their particular interests, even if that means, in the extreme, murder and genocide.

I was to find out very quickly that even amid my own religious and political circle, the issue of trust was to become pivotal in the preservation of my own life, and yes, even my very soul!

One last item of information will round out the context of my adventure.

The High Priest, a fellow Pharisee, was traditionally a person of direct decent from the family of Aaron.

It follows that approval of the person aspiring to that position, notwithstanding their ancestral claim to the position, demanded every effort to appease Roman rule by any means possible. And in all fairness, the Sanhedrin as a whole walked the tightrope between legitimate religious/political responsibilities and the authority of our enemy.

Could that suggest a compromise with the Governor in bringing to heal subversive Jewish elements set on disrupting or even ending Roman rule?

Even more disturbing, could bribery be involved in assuring some satisfactory status within the Roman/Judeo administration of the nation?

Why not add a further complication to the equation?

I speak of Herod the Tetrarch who was then a "puppet" king. He was son of the first Herod who some thirty-one years before had slaughtered all the male children of two years of age or under, throughout Bethlehem and region. This was an attempt to eliminate a baby called "Jesus" who he thought could be a future pretender to his throne; the same Jesus of Nazareth I write about.

Pilate, the Roman Governor, had relegated this second Herod to a governorship in Galilee, in an attempt to appease the sensitivities of supporters of Jewish royalty; not to mention the convenience of keeping the "King" out of his way. This decision made the two men livid enemies.

You will read more about Herod further into my story.

I can assure you that the influence of any of these elements, with their subsequent riches, position and power, could be sufficient to render impotent any spiritual resolve that a human soul might aspire to. I know, because my adventure brought me face-to-face with all of them.

CHAPTER 3

Decision Time

WHY ON EARTH would I embark on a journey that I knew full well could bring my world crashing down around me? In fact, that one night could strip away a lifetime of achievement; to say nothing of the damage it could do to my family.

But seldom do we ever find our lives to be within our absolute control. Life seems to bring circumstances and pressures to which we are constantly adjusting.

In particular, core values expressed in our religion, politics, career, family, social concerns, and most certainly one's personal spiritual convictions, are often challenged by events that sweep whole societies into utter chaos, and leave "every man for himself" as the saying has it.

That's just where I eventually found myself! In the loneliest moment of my life! Bereft of any tangible support! Not even my wife and family, nor my closest friends could share in the decision that confronted me.

Let me explain!

Our nation, Israel, had risen out of four hundred and thirty years of slavery to the king of Egypt. In that time our people had cried out to God. They begged him to deliver them from bondage.

Finally he did, through his servant Moses who led them to within view of the land God had promised to Abraham, founder of our nation.

Joshua, his successor actually led them into that land in glorious victory over numerous enemies.

Over the process of time, we had fallen repeatedly into enemy hands, notably the Babylonians; then the Persians; and finally here we were under the domination of yet a third conqueror, The Roman Empire.

Throughout those turbulent years God had spoken to us through numerous prophets preaching repentance and a return to the principles and practices of our faith that Moses had received directly from the very hand of God on Mount Sinai.

Our history plainly demonstrates the place of godliness and piety in the wellbeing of a nation, and conversely, the insufferable consequences of our backslidings.

Throughout our history, indeed from the dawn of creation to now, there was identified a theme, indeed a revelation, of a Messiah, a deliverer who would come and set us free from all tyranny.

Never before had we been so poised, as we were now, to expect that deliverance.

Then came a roughshod boisterous itinerant preacher, by the name of John the Baptist, to the Jordan River to call our people to repentance of their sins, announcing the immanent coming of the promised Messiah.

John was the first prophetic voice our nation had heard in over four hundred years since Malachi the Prophet, whose writings comprise the final words of the Old Testament of the Bible.

Great crowds of our people made a pilgrimage to the Jordan River to be baptized by the evangelist for the remission of sins.

His preaching was most effective, and the common people heard him gladly, and responded to the opportunity for personal spiritual solace, having long ago abandoned the religious rituals of the temple and synagogue, from which they had in any case been largely excluded. They were truly a flock without a shepherd.

The popularity of the evangelist posed a serious threat to the religious authority vested in the Scribes and Pharisees. But who could gainsay the adulation of the common people, so spiritually hungry, if they found no solace in their religion?

It seemed to many of the Sanhedrin, both Pharisees and Sadducees, that as the expression has it, "If you can't lick 'em, join 'em!" In any case, would the general populace not commend us for such a pious act of baptism, as a sign of our identity with their spiritual needs?

Well, that did it! John would have none of it. He saw right through the charade. "You brood of vipers!" Have you ever been called such a thing? Well, that's how he addressed us, whether present or no.

To be fair, John was not barring any of us from sincere repentance of our sins. But, to use another vernacular, he "hit the nail on the head." Were we truly interested in the needs of our own soul? Or was our confidence solely in our position and authority within our religious structure? I suspect it was the latter.

But the full exposé was yet to come, and would lead to the darkest period in our national history!

"I and my Father are one."

(John 10:30;)

CHAPTER 4

Enough Is Enough

THE MINISTRY OF John the Baptist had already been the main agenda of the Sanhedrin for some time, where precious little support was forthcoming for his message, given his uncompromising attitude toward his religious leaders.

But the bombshell came when he declared that a man called Jesus, of Nazareth in Galilee, was the long expected Messiah of Israel, a claim that would demand of us the most pertinent examination of his credentials.

John's declaration brought further distress, in that his claim was based upon a vision he had supposedly received by which he was to know the identity of the Messiah. He would see the anointing Holy Spirit descend upon God's chosen one.

He adamantly declared that when he had performed the baptism of Jesus he saw the Spirit descend and rest on him in the form of a dove, and that he heard a heavenly voice declare, "This is my beloved Son, in whom I am well pleased. Hear ye him."

Despite the usual large crowd that had gathered to hear John, only he and Jesus heard and understood the annunciation that was given. But the hundreds gathered there would ever declare that, as Jesus ascended from the river, the clouds parted emitting a brilliant ray of light upon him, and an immense, almost deafening sound, like thunder, came from the source of that light.

It didn't help matters that he then disappeared for some forty days. Evidently he retreated to a desert place, probably to think through the implications of the ministry he felt called to.

Afterward he showed up in Galilee, his home province, and settled in Capernaum at the head of the Sea of Galilee. But that was not the last we were to hear of him.

By John's own admission, Jesus was to succeed him in his ministry of evangelism. But no one was prepared for the radical change he would bring to Israel and beyond. In fact his ministry would exceed anything we had ever known from the early prophets to the present moment of time.

Surely we all could applaud his extraordinary powers to heal the sick and exorcise demon-possessed people. For sure his reported raising of the dead required some careful scrutiny; and the influence he commanded over the masses was unprecedented in all our religious history.

But there's the rub. These religiously disenfranchised people hung on every word he said.

To complicate things further, he was addressing them in the local synagogues, wherever he went; until the crowds simply required that he hold outdoor rallies, usually by the seashore, using a boat as his platform due to the pressing crowd, and to produce the necessary amplification that voice-over-water achieves.

Double rub! Once again we Pharisees were the center of criticism, similar to that of John. But Jesus' criticism seemed to us to become unusually vehement.

He was equally as familiar with the Jewish Scriptures as we were, in fact complimenting us on our careful study of the Law of Moses, considered to be the basis of Jewish faith and practice, and contained in our most holy book the Torah.

However, to his mind we were guilty of turning and twisting these laws to our favor and convenience, so that the keeping of them became impossible to those of lesser social and religious standing.

In fact we had gone to such extremes as to create another book of rules called the Talmud, supposedly to enable Jews to keep the law with greater accuracy. It was not long before this second book took precedence over the first, giving the Sanhedrin total control over the very souls of the populace, while at the same time, denying them any spiritual relief.

Triple rub! The general public gladly heard what Jesus had to say, because he offered them a personal relationship with God, based upon his claim to be the Messiah, the Son of God. They need only believe this, and upon his personal authority vested in him by the Creator, their sins were forgiven and they were assured of eternal salvation.

He offered his miracles of healing, exorcism and the raising of the dead as proof of his divine authority, effectively bringing into question the authenticity of what was held to be the greatest religious institution of our time!

To top things off, he claimed to be the champion of our religion, even the very fulfillment of its prophetical teachings.

Clearly enough was enough! This man had to be stopped! That "dark and stormy night" you've been waiting to read about was now as unstoppable as he was. And I was right in the middle of the whole drama.

*"...Who do people say the
Son of Man is?"*

(Matthew 16: 13;)

CHAPTER 5

From Nazareth Yet

JESUS OF NAZARETH! Jesus of Nazareth! Jesus of Nazareth! Would
that name never cease to be the lead item on the agenda of every
session of the Sanhedrin?

"How in God's name (the uttering of such was considered
by us to be blasphemous) was the business of our nation to be
advanced?"

But that was the point. This Jesus fellow had no compunction
about using the name of God in his discourses, claiming that God
was in fact the Father of all mankind, whether Jew or Gentile,
effectively providing the commoner of our race with direct
access to, and personal relationship with God as their "Heavenly
Father."

Throughout his ministry, that lasted only three years, he
repeatedly referred to himself as, "the son of man," in deference
to his earthly ancestry as the son of Joseph and Mary. That made
him a direct descendant of King David, a fact that could not be
disputed.

But to suggest that God was his father, and by deduction
our father, flew in the face of our most cherished claim to be,
exclusively, the chosen people of God as the "Sons of Abraham,"
the founder of our nation, chosen by God himself.

From time immemorial we Jews had always called ourselves such. He was always referred to as "Father Abraham."

Now, add to that his lineage, from which our future Messiah was thought to come; and given his miraculous powers, it is little wonder that the total populace was asking out loud, "Is Jesus the Messiah for whom we have so long waited?"

Talk about a "thorn in the flesh." This man Jesus was much more than that. He was a threat to any and all expressions of authority. And we're not just talking about the institutions of law, politics, or religion. We are talking people! Those of us who stood to suffer devastating loss should the institutional framework fail!

That's when the threat became really personal. Every member of the Sanhedrin had an enormous vested interest in the "Jesus Question."

That's when the age-old enigma of politics reared its ugly head: the power struggle!

Our political system was more complicated because of the lack of democratic process in our form of government, and doubly complicated because our authority was subjected to the whims of Roman occupation.

Every session of our assembly would present seventy-two people with a very personal dilemma. "What will *I* do with Jesus?"

*"...If they keep quiet, the
stones will cry out."*

(Luke 19:40;)

CHAPTER 6

The Problem

I<small>T WAS A</small> session I will never forget!

Oh, we had been debating the Jesus problem for the last three
years, spasmodically at first. But his increasing popularity made it
imperative that we take a firmer grip on the question.

Neither was it all done behind closed doors. We had
sometimes sent delegations from the Sanhedrin to wherever he
was preaching.

This became somewhat of a sparring game with Jesus.
Our lawyers and priests would quite often challenge him with
questions that really only held interest for us Pharisees. But Jesus
would win the argument every time. Score: Jesus all! – Pharisees
zilch! Well, fair is fair!

But then, he would, in front of us, tell the people to listen to
what we had to say, but in no wise were they to live as we lived,
an assumption that we did not practice what we preached.

Finally, he began to criticize our traditions, not the law, mind
you, but certainly the Talmud. He openly criticized our conduct,
and in particular, our interpretation of the law. He accused us of
being totally self-serving and a threat to the spiritual welfare of
the masses.

Clearly, things had gotten out of hand. Something had to be
done, and quickly.

Jesus and his disciples had come to Jerusalem, presumably to observe the Passover, the most important religious observance of our nation. But what an entry! The most pompous visit to Jerusalem, including King Herod himself, never garnered a crowd like he had that day.

Word spread like wildfire that Jesus was on his way into the city. Droves of pilgrims from all over Israel and surrounding countries accompanied him as he made his way from Bethany, the route becoming more and more crowded as folks from Jerusalem scurried out of the city to line the road that Jesus and his disciples were traveling.

It was enough to alert the Roman garrison for crowd control; the more urgent because of possible bands of Jewish loyalists, more frequent of late, bent on riot and insurrection that hopefully would lead to the overthrow of our Roman enemies.

But what they saw was anything but an insurrection. In fact the smirk on their Roman faces, even outright laughter, greeted Jesus' entourage, because here he came into view riding on the colt of a donkey.

The people were spreading their outer garments and even palm branches on the road for Jesus to ride over, and wildly shouting and singing praises to God for the arrival of their Messiah. "Blessed is the king who comes in the name of the Lord! Peace in heaven and glory in the highest!"

That got our attention, I'll tell you! Neither us Pharisees nor the Sadducees were smirking, much less laughing. Here was the very enactment of the prophecy of Zechariah.

"Rejoice greatly, O Daughter of Zion! Shout, Daughter of Jerusalem! See your king comes to you, righteous and having salvation, gentle and riding a donkey, on a colt, the foal of a donkey."

This had to be dealt with right on the spot. Some of our Pharisee members made a dash for the road and demanded that Jesus tell his disciples and the crowd to "knock it off," as the current expression has it. Jesus replied, "I tell you, if they keep quiet, the stones will cry out."

The procession ended at the Temple Gate. Jesus got off the colt and entered the building. He took one look around the place where merchants were selling sheep and doves to the celebrants, and moneychangers were converting Roman coins into temple money, for a fee of course!

Then, utter chaos!

To our surprise, Jesus, using a makeshift whip, proceeded to drive the animals from their stalls, release the doves from their cages, and turned over the tables of the moneychangers, scattering coins in every direction.

In a loud voice, with his finger pointed right at us Pharisees, he shouted *"It is written my house will be a house of prayer but you have made it a den of robbers."*

Fortunately, he then left the building and the city, and apparently went to stay with friends in the neighboring town of Bethany, leaving the commerce of the day in complete disarray.

But that wasn't the end of him. He was back the next day, teaching the common people in the Temple atrium.

We decided we would challenge him as to what authority was invested in him to do and say these things.

Jesus simply turned the table on us by asking where John The Baptist got his authority to baptize people at the river Jordan, among them a number of the Pharisees: From Heaven or from men?

He had us cornered, because the people believed John to be a prophet, in fact, as he himself claimed to be, the forerunner of the Messiah. To answer that John's authority came from the Temple authority would insight a riot for sure.

So much for questions! He wasn't going to answer that one!

In fact we continually put our best religious and legal minds into the crowd to take issue with his teaching, but they were no match for this rabbi.

We finally got Rome into the discussion by asking if it was right for us to pay taxes to Caesar, as though to accuse him of cheating the Roman Government.

Of all the red faces in the crowd, ours couldn't have been more scarlet! He simply asked for a coin and then asked whose image appeared on the coin. Of course it was that of Caesar. "Then give to Caesar what is Caesar's." Then came the clincher: "And give to God what is God's."

We all knew that our compromise with the Romans and mutual suppression of the common people had produced loopholes in our religious practices so that we most conveniently cheated both God and State.

No more open questions! Ever!

That Passover week was the most tedious I have ever experienced as my colleagues and I were faced with personal, professional, religious and ethical questions that would nag at our souls until dealt with.

But I digress!

CHAPTER 7

Pedigrees

As I was saying, there we sat in emergency session, one item only on the agenda - What would we do with Jesus?

There had been considerable interaction with Jesus by a number of Pharisees, and even some of the Sadducees, enough to bring into the discussion varied assessments of the man.

Given that there seemed to be no violation of legal issues we could charge him with, the discussion was repeatedly boiling down to the same personal question: What would *I* do with Jesus?

Clearly, there would be no majority consensus forthcoming! The Sanhedrin was already divided between religious/doctrinal issues. And now amongst ourselves we Pharisees were also divided in our assessment of Jesus.

But then, under our form of government "consensus" counted for very little. The fact that supreme authority rested with the High Priest, further complicated by the hereditary nature of that office, the supposedly "democratic" process was truly a façade.

In this instance Annas was High Priest emeritus, five of his sons in succession having held that office, and he still held the office of Chief of the Sanhedrin, even though Caiaphas, his son-in-law, was then acting High Priest.

Open debate was in reality pretentious!

O yes, opinions could be liberally expressed but, in the end, the debate always acquiesced to the will of the High Priest. To take any other position was, at best, to jeopardize one's influence in the Sanhedrin, and worse, one's membership in that prestigious body, not to mention the public disgrace that would precipitate.

To be sure, there were some of our members who secretly believed Jesus to be the promised Messiah, or at the very least gave credence to his benevolent ministry. But alas! Conviction always gave way to fear, and there was none who would stand in his defense.

I managed to pluck up enough courage to suggest that under our law no man should be convicted before he had opportunity to defend himself.

With scorn, Caiaphas suggested I might also have come from Galilee, a region commonly noted for its troublesome lower class citizens, unworthy of the attention of the elite.

Even the disciple Nathanael, when invited to meet Jesus of Nazareth for the first time, was heard to remark, "Can any good thing come out of Nazareth?"

It was clear to my mind that Jesus didn't stand a chance.

But I sat in utter shock when Caiaphas stated plainly that it would be actually expedient for Jesus to be put to death, rather than for the whole nation to suffer the consequences of a supposed insurrection (he was later charged with) that could lead to the annihilation of the Jewish state at the hands of the Romans.

He could not know it then, but Caiaphas had pronounced the fulfillment of the ancient prophecy that Jesus would in fact die for the Jewish nation as a propitiation for the sins of the whole world.

There it was! Plain and unmistakable! A plot to justify the death of Jesus, the only hope we had of a voice from God, after four hundred years of prophetic silence.

The unholy shame that hung so heavily over that room! Guilt that wafted from one soul to the other in that assembly! We were without doubt the ones who were already on trial here.

As swiftly as possible Jesus would stand before us on the so-called scale of justice; and all our combined fame, wealth, authority, prestige and power on the other side of that scale could never tip it one iota in our favor.

I slinked home in devastating silence, crushed by my cowardly decision to place my good fortune ahead of the death of an innocent man.

"God help me!" I don't know if it was a prayer, or simply a sigh of defeat.

If I had any conscience at all, I must do the only thing left for me to do. I must see for myself who it was I had, by my silence, condemned to death.

I must take that walk into the night!

CHAPTER 8

Tread Carefully

T HERE WERE A number of steps that had to be taken before and during my journey. It would involve a number of people. The question was, "Who could I trust?"

To begin with, I had to discern who in the Sanhedrin were in some way favorably impressed with Jesus, or even sympathized with his precarious position with us. They would be needed to back me up if I might find evidence enough to speak favorably on his behalf.

Furthermore, it was rumored that one or more of our members might have a contact with the disciples of Jesus.

I would need such assistance, as there was no possible way I could make personal contact with Jesus without arousing the suspicion of Jesus' group and the Sanhedrin.

It was thought that Jesus' disciple John was known personally to the High Priest, presumably because he had first been a disciple of John the Baptist and, after the Baptist's imprisonment, he and his brother James had joined with Jesus in his ministry.

So there might be some way we could get word to John that I sought a meeting with Jesus. But best that the inquiry come from some other member of the Sanhedrin that I could trust, so as to cover my tracks. That my sham defense of Jesus at our last meeting had already put suspicion upon me was quite clear.

Joseph of Arimathea, or even so respected a member as Gamaliel, might know some willing servant of the household of the High Priest who could get a message to John, were he or she sympathetic toward Jesus.

I am glad to say that a connection was made, although the details of such an arrangement must remain a mystery for all time.

I knew the meeting would have to be held outside the city walls because Jesus and his disciples retired from the city each day after their teaching appearances in the Temple vestibule. This would constitute my next challenge.

I was on friendly terms with the Centurion, leader of the Temple Guard the Romans provided for the safety of members of the Sanhedrin. He was totally indifferent to our current concerns for this Jesus fellow. Were I to ask his assistance in my passage to parts outside the city, such would be considered routine, since he was responsible for my personal safety in any case, no matter the time of day or night.

Therein lies the clue to my next challenge. Such a meeting would most certainly have to take place under the cover of darkness. Furthermore, my Roman escort would somehow have to be limited to my passing through the city gate at night. To the disciples there must in nowise be even a hint of Roman involvement in my plans.

Could my riches perhaps find some more justifiable use in securing their cooperation? I leave any presumptions to your imagination.

Finally, how would anyone find one's way to Jesus' hiding place?

And what a hiding place it was! Jesus knew full well that he was a marked man, subject to arrest, or even assassination, if he made just one careless move.

Then how could anyone associated with him be seen in my company, much less with a compliment of Roman soldiers?

It was well known that the Jesus group frequented the Mount of Olives on the other side of the Kidron Valley.

It was a most popular venue for tourists and local picnic groups who frequented the famous Olive Groves that clung to its slopes. But there were more secluded parts to the mountain that were largely unknown to the general public, ideal for the privacy of Jesus and his disciples.

Question! How would we arrange to make contact once I was outside the city gate?

"Back to the drawing board," as the old saying has it. There was nothing for it but to further prevail upon those same Sanhedrin members who might arrange contact with John in the first place, knowing full well that without trust betrayal would turn the whole scheme into disaster.

By the process of elimination, first off my list was any of the Sadducees.

To begin with, they cared not a whit for Jesus' claims to any spiritual motivation whatsoever, given their stand against a life hereafter and their dismissal of any thought of resurrection from the dead.

To their minds, he was nothing more than a political upstart.

Furthermore, they relished any and all opportunity to discredit us Pharisees and weaken our hold on the political agenda that our majority in the Sanhedrin afforded us.

Just find one Pharisee who was ready to secretly oppose the will of the High Priest, and there would be enough "tar and feather" to paint all of us as incompetent to rule under Roman occupation, thus establishing their sect as the only viable alternative.

I chose Joseph of Arimathea, just based on my own instincts (or so I thought at the time). Something about his demeanor in the Sanhedrin discussions of the Jesus question strongly impressed me.

Here was a true statesman of Israel. A man who was held in great respect by his peers and the common people alike, despite his riches and political power.

He was a godly man, most pious in his religious observances, yet never aloof to the needs of the lower classes.

He was even held in great respect by the Roman authorities throughout Judea, and I suspect his influence reached even into the lofty realm of Rome itself.

In fact, of all men in the Sanhedrin, I thought him to have the most influence with the High Priest, if only to inflict on this potentate an unwelcome discomfort.

Joseph sought no accolades from any man, but his religious influence was without doubt the strongest among his peers.

I would tell him of my plans to go to Jesus, and seek his help to contact John.

I thought it only fair to also reveal to him my hope that he would accompany me beyond the city gates to dissuade any suspicion of my meeting with the disciple.

Should he not agree, it was likely that the game was over before it started, taking my career and respectability with it.

I pondered if it was appropriate that I invite Joseph to my home on a social basis, and there spring the question on him.

Or, perhaps he would agree to see me in the privacy of his own home here in Jerusalem.

I opted for this latter plan, to which he was most cordial.

Suffice to say, the meeting did take place and, much to my relief, he was in total agreement with my plan.

He knew a Jesus sympathizer in the household staff of Caiaphas. He would ask him to make contact with John on my behalf. He would also arrange a small entourage to accompany us just outside the city walls, dismissing the Roman guards once they had cleared our passage through the gate.

On the pretense of some private matter, he would accompany me alone to some point prearranged with John, just beyond their notice. He would then return to his friends explaining that I had encountered others who would accompany me to my destination, so he was no longer needed.

Well then, it only remained for John to send a message to me as to what night and time he would take me to Jesus.

If only it were that simple!

This meeting must take place in private! No ifs, ands, or buts! That is to say, not even any of Jesus' disciples, other than John, must know of our plans. I did think it likely that Peter would have to be told, since he was the presumed lieutenant to Jesus. In any case, it would be wise to hold our discussions in the presence of two witnesses. Besides, Peter could dispel any concern amongst the other ten, should they get wind of our meeting, given that they had been told by Jesus that he had actually come to Jerusalem to die at the hands of his own people.

Neither they, nor myself could have known that Judas Iscariot, one of the twelve, was seeking opportunity to betray his Master to the Sanhedrin. Had he known of my plans, he would have gone straightway to the Chief Priest with his accusations and believe me there might well have been four crosses on Golgotha that eventful morning.

So that meant that a place, other than where the disciples commonly met, would have to be found.

I did not know until later that Jesus himself picked the spot. Nor was I to know that spot was to be the most sacred place that ever imprinted the footsteps of man.

Time was running out! It was only a matter of days, if not hours, before Caiaphas would send a detachment of soldiers and a few of his closest colleagues to arrest Jesus. He needed only to find out Jesus' hiding place.

Though I didn't know it then, my race was not with the High Priest; it was with Judas!

"...whoever comes to me I will never drive away."

(John 6:37;)

CHAPTER 9

Response

JOSEPH MUST HAVE convinced John of the urgency of the meeting because his response came even more quickly than I had hoped.

We had no problem with our arrangement with the Roman guard (provided my bribe was not discovered) and our entourage was readily assembled. The point of meeting with John was determined.

But the most important part of our planning I haven't mentioned yet!

Have you ever embarked on some venture you thought appropriate, when at the last moment you ask yourself, "What on earth am I doing?" But too late! You can't back out now. You kind of take a gulp, straighten the shoulders and plunge headlong into whatever awaits you?

Ditto!

Only this time for me, physical plans had so preoccupied my mind and time that I had given little thought to the course of my conversation with Jesus.

To begin with, why was I involving myself with this man at all? Wasn't he just the son of a carpenter from a nondescript town called Nazareth?

Well that was the problem; he was far more than that! We all knew it, despite our despicable and deliberate attempts to

33

diminish his ministry in a hypocritical charade to "save the country and our religion."

As if even the greatest of our religious traditions could stand superior to the healing of the sick; the raising of the dead; and the restoring of spiritual hope to the people! How ridiculous could we be?

I tried to convince myself that the reason for my visit was to warn Jesus to get out of town *now*! Not a bad reason at all.

But I knew in my heart this was not the reason why I was going.

Was I going to change sides, align myself with Jesus and hopefully raise an army to crush our Roman conquerors?

No! I knew from repeated attempts of other zealots that such was useless. The latest casualty had been another Jesus, Jesus Barabbas, presently in Roman custody awaiting execution. I certainly had no stomach for yet another one, much less one who made no offence whatever except to offer his amazing gifts to the needy out of his obvious love for mankind.

Only a genuine personal reason for such a meeting would cut it with Jesus of Nazareth.

Such a reason there was!

I had only to admit it to myself, weigh the cost of my action, and drop the pretense of representing the Sanhedrin. I was going for *me*! No one else!

It hit me hard! Here were seventy-two men, all party to a plot of *murder*! And I was one of them! How could a lifetime of religious conviction and service to God and his chosen people have come to this?

No! I had no intention of making any commitment to the Nazarene or to the plot of the Sanhedrin. I guess at that late hour I wasn't sure it was rationale or emotion that was driving me. But one thing was sure; I was seeking a way out of the impending crisis, for myself as much as for Jesus.

If he would back off his attacks on us, it might be that the two sides could come to a position of compromise, and both he, and myself in particular, could avoid a catastrophic situation.

In my naivety I could not possibly have comprehended the raw rancor that is precipitated by pride, greed, ambition and power, even within religious circles. But I was soon to find out!

So, to set the agenda!

Openers are always important. Sometimes to state the obvious can make a handy compliment. "I'll just acknowledge his powers as those given by God himself." So I told myself.

Then I thought, "I'll let him know the danger he could be in if the quarrel between his group and ours could not be fixed."

Further, I would admit to him that there were others in the Sanhedrin sympathetic to his work. At least they were ready to join me in giving him a fair hearing.

Finally, I would give him a chance to help me to better understand the philosophy of his ministry, hoping that would benefit us religious leaders and the populace as a whole.

"Nicodemus! You poor impoverished soul!" I might have just as well said it out loud!

I didn't know it then, but the agenda would be all his!

In fact, after that meeting, I would never be the same again!

Yes, I at least could admit that I was going for "me." But I had no idea how much I needed it. Nor could I know its eternal consequences.

I was to learn on one dark and stormy night what really happens when a soul meets Jesus, head-to-head, heart-to-heart, and soul-to-soul.

"...Who is my mother, and who are my brothers?"

(Matthew 12:48;)

CHAPTER 10

The Family

WHERE WAS MY family in all of this, you ask? Good question! In fact up to this point they knew nothing of my plans, much less my heart in this matter.

Of course, even though some of the children were of adult age, and of those still at home, some in higher grades at school, they could never be party to my present business.

Considered a man at thirteen years of age, the male teenagers certainly were active with their fathers in the synagogue at various stages of their bar mitzvah. Even so, at my level of status in the religious and political affairs of our country, my responsibilities demanded of me complete privacy.

The women of Jewry had no status whatever in religious affairs. Nonetheless, my faithful and pious wife was a true gift to a man of my station.

She was privy to many aspects of my responsibilities. I found relief in sharing with her some of my burdens about public life.

She made no secret of her pride and admiration of her husband, to me or to our friends and associates, but I assure you she never once gossiped to others about my work.

Now, on the eve of my adventure, it was necessary to share with her the cause of my impending absence, given that it might be well into the night, even daylight, before my return – if I got home at all!

Even then I just could not share with her the agony of my heart in personal terms. To do so would have threatened her own commitment to our nation and to her religious faith.

A sensible and even courageous attempt at restoring justice for this Jesus fellow, if justified, she could understand and accept.

She well knew the dangers of traveling outside the safety of the city walls at night. But she was somewhat comforted by the presence of the Roman guard; (I dared not tell her of their limited role). Plus, although she did not know my destination, I had assured her that the distance of my travel was not extreme.

She did surprise me as to her rather substantial understanding of the current events surrounding Jesus and his entourage, garnered I think from the incessant cackle of the women in the marketplace; the whole city by now fairly exploding with ideas as to the final outcome of the Jesus episode.

And I was secretly pleased with her compassionate attitude toward the man, her tender heart no doubt moved by the tales of many healings and even exorcisms. To be honest, she was somewhat jaundiced to the tales of his raising the dead.

But now the hour of my departure was at hand. We embraced, and she wished me well, promising that her prayers would follow me. Any inquiries from the family, young or old, would be met with the usual casual references to the many demands of Sanhedrin and temple duties that were mine.

With that, I stepped out into the night!

"...For all who draw the sword will die by the sword."

(Matthew 26:52;)

CHAPTER 11

On Our Way

I CANNOT ADEQUATELY SHARE with you the turmoil of my emotions as my adventure began. Excitement? Yes! Fear? Noticeably so! Concern for the mission? "In spades," as the common vernacular has it!

But these emotions were largely veneered by the minute particulars of the journey.

As I closed the door behind me a small detail of my Roman bodyguard met me and escorted me toward the eastern gate of the city. Joseph and his band met us part way.

Concerned for the privacy of my journey, the Centurion ordered his detail of men to await him at a point out of sight of the gate. He then ordered the gatekeepers to open the needle gate, large enough for only one person to pass through at a time. This prevented any rushing the main gate by marauding bandits, or more pertinently, Jewish zealots.

The coast was clear! No sensible person, Jew or Gentile, was to be seen on a night like this, much less outside the security of the city walls.

It was only then that I noticed the cutting wind of the impending storm that loomed in the distance. It swept multiple clouds repeatedly across the starry heavens, so common this time of year, and conveniently hid the shining moon from our cautious party as we progressed down the hard and noisome pavement of excellent engineered Roman roads.

The main gate of the city was just out of view when our party met John, accompanied by his brother James, and as one might have guessed, Peter also. They stood in the shadows at the juncture of an unpaved road, more a path than a thoroughfare.

None of the disciples were distinguishable to Joseph's party in the poor light of the few lanterns we had brought with us.

I uttered a rather pretentious exclamation of surprise as to our encounter so the meeting would not appear to have been planned. I explained to Joseph that the three men were friends of mine and were headed in the same direction as myself. There would be no need for further inconveniencing of himself and his friends!

The journey continued, I to my encounter with Jesus, and Joseph and his group back to the waiting Roman escort at the city gate.

At this point I turned my full attention to the three men into whose hands I had entrusted myself, with no inclination as to what they were thinking about this moment, except to follow the instructions of their Lord.

Although my immediate assessment of them was consistent with what I would imagine three fishermen to be, I was certainly aware of the distinctiveness of each personality.

John, for all his masculinity, was a man who oozed great sensitivity. To learn that this man was the closest confidant of Jesus brings no surprise, given his depth of feeling and powers of observation betrayed by his eyes.

He struck me as being a man that would not "sweat the small stuff," as the saying has it, being willing to take a back seat to those who by instinct or ambition took hold of a leadership role. But I marked him as one whose loyalty to his convictions and to Jesus could never be questioned.

He undoubtedly was eager to please if the matter matched his sensitivities.

Being the closest of the disciples to Jesus, John enjoyed an intimate friendship with him.

I suspect he likely was party to Jesus' deepest confidences.

For certain, he was most concerned for the safety and wellbeing of his Rabbi, and I sensed that he had only acquiesced to arrange my meeting with the hope that it would bring some sort of relief from the threats of the Sanhedrin.

To reflect, I think he may well have been impressed that there was one possible ally amid that den of power brokers.

He certainly must be in similar straights as myself, having to exercise blind trust that I would keep all counsel and circumstances of this venture to myself.

Now James was almost unreadable! The quietude of his persona was completely contradictory to the physical demands of his occupation. Yet, I detected an alertness that was betrayed in the set of his jaw and the intense restlessness of his eyes. "He didn't miss a thing," so his demeanor seemed to say. And even in this initial encounter I could tell he was the consummate bodyguard to his brother John.

He spoke not a word. But then those more intimate with the twelve disciples always admitted that James was the "quiet" one amongst the band.

He certainly had the full confidence of Jesus, and I assessed that he was valuable to Jesus in opinionating the conversations of others, whether he was personally involved or not.

Then there was Peter!

It seemed immediately to me that there was "always Peter." He was massive in physique, though certainly not fat. Every muscle was poised and alert to his every move.

Though I could not confirm my next impression by word by reason of his silence, I knew immediately that here was the leader of this team.

He was, without question, one who, despite my illustrious position in life, I would be compelled to follow rather than to confront him. But I thought his "bigger than life personality" somehow masked a certain natural insecurity.

This may have been planned as a meeting with John, but there was no way of getting there without Peter's approval.

I can assure you that not a word was exchanged between us. But looks were sufficient! I could tell he disapproved of this visit, and he was big enough and eager enough to end it promptly by force if necessary. I was surprised to see that he carried a sword discretely covered by his vestments.

Only the agreement of Jesus to the meeting, and his insistence that he accompany John to meet me, would make Peter acquiesce to it.

Well, my personal observations of the three not withstanding, I was sure glad I had them as my escort, because they would have been a ready defense against robbers or other intruders.

But back to the journey!

John assured me that James and Peter were no threat to our plans, as these three were considered by the other disciples to be inseparable, and they were party to the more secluded locale of our meeting, unknown to the other nine disciples.

John led us up a rather steep, narrow path as we climbed the Mount of Olives. It was surprisingly well hidden from the view below, or from above. It was the trail commonly used by Jesus when he sought seclusion from the crowds that doted on his teaching, or more accurately his miracles.

John further explained it led to that part of the mountain that was virtually unknown to the frequent hikers that roamed the many paths. Only these three disciples had ever been there with Jesus, and very rarely at that.

It was Jesus' frequent habit to rise early in the morning, long before daylight, when he would head for this spot to pray. It was, they said, the place where Jesus prepared himself to meet the eager crowds he would encounter each day. And, from where he never came down but what his face shone with a glow of such serenity. And his voice, yes his whole persona, exuded a heart of love and compassion that the disciples envied, but were never able to duplicate, until one memorable occasion yet to come.

But I am getting ahead of myself!

As we neared the summit of the mountain, the terrain proved quite steep, and I admit to some fatigue as we approached our destination. But of course my three escorts were taking the heights "in stride" literally. Countless miles of travel with an itinerant preacher had certainly honed their bodies to peak condition.

With each step my anxiety level overtook my excitement at the thought of meeting Jesus, peaking to near dread as I realized the imminent moment that was almost upon me. Never before in my experience had my elite persona been so quickly reduced to being a very ordinary common man.

Where was I going? Why was I going? How was I getting there? These held no candescence whatever to *whom* I was going.

Abruptly ending my reverie, Peter suddenly brushed aside a bramble of branches that seemed to block the trail. The journey was over!

As we stepped beyond this natural gateway to the place of meeting my heart was noticeably pounding, not only from exertion, but also from my anticipation of finally meeting Jesus in a personal encounter.

We had reached the place called Gethsemane!

"Take my yoke upon you and learn from me,…"

(Matthew 11:29;)

CHAPTER 12

Look Who's Talking

We certainly had climbed a good distance above the public paths that inundated this beautiful mountain with its numerous olive groves.

The clearing I walked into was not large. Conceivably it would accommodate perhaps four to six people who might recline under the spreading boughs of shade trees that easily blocked any view or intrusion from the higher elevations of the mountain. The lower bushes formed a solid wall all around it, effectively guaranteeing privacy. No one could ever have found it, even by accident. Like me, they would have had to be led there! And they would be! Its location would have to be compromised by someone familiar with it. And it would be!

To my left was a narrow, fairly long path that John said led to a substantial encampment where the larger company of disciples, their wives, and other devoted women, met and attended to the needs of the group. It was similarly hidden from any public attention, and this adjoining path was used, by mutual consent, only at the invitation of Jesus.

But where did Jesus seclude himself when necessary? I was soon to find out!

To the right of our entry was a fairly nondescript opening that led to a much smaller glen, quite remote from the others, but ideal for an intimate meeting of just three or four people.

The path was somewhat stony, but it gave way to a flat rock surface that increased in layers until it formed a ledge about chair height, ideal for sitting upon. The floor of the area was pleasantly covered with soft moss that even cushioned some of the reclining areas with its comfort.

I noticed in a more remote corner a large rock; worn quite smooth; It was bare, as though it had borne the discipline of the ages. It was strangely marked in spots with what appeared to be streaks of stain lighter than the natural hue of the rock. Surrounded by the moss floor of the clearing, it gave me an uncanny mental picture of a naturally configured altar. Could it possibly be his place of prayer?

And there he was! Jesus!

It was at that point that the three disciples left us, and we were free to familiarize ourselves one with the other.

Obviously it was to be "Me first!"

There he stood, rather nondescript in physical features, save that he was much weather tanned with an obviously strong physique. There were no airs about him. He was not in the least threatening in his tone of voice or his mannerisms. For all his strength he appeared most gentle, warm and friendly.

Yet, there was a certain graveness about him that gave me the impression that he carried heavy responsibilities upon his shoulders. Perhaps some concern for the course of our meeting?

Believe me, that preposition was very quickly dispelled!

He gave no hint of notice to our diametrically opposite backgrounds, notwithstanding my position in society. I was just another human soul on his agenda, but it became immediately apparent that I was his sole focus.

I was instantly impressed by a sense of genuine love that exuded from his demeanor. His voice was soft and deep as though emanating from deep within his spirit; you know, that part of a person that one seems to connect with up front, before all other assessments.

Without fanfare he bade me sit down, and then sat quietly facing me, his eyes totally consuming me. They were so deep; so gentle; so wise; so loving; so accepting!

To my surprise, I felt completely at ease.

Whatever my agenda, his only agenda was me! I knew instinctively this moment was to be pivotal in my human journey!

He waited for me to open the conversation. There was no impatience; no frustration conveyed in his face. He seemed genuinely intent on whatever I would say, whenever I might choose to say it.

Almost involuntarily the words came, and I said, "Rabbi, we know you are a teacher who has come from God. For no one could perform the miraculous signs you are doing if God were not with him."

Instantly I knew, a more damning statement I could have never made!

Intended to be complimentary, I had completely contradicted the position that we of the Sanhedrin held, that he was a charlatan, and I had just exposed myself to a withering rebuke for such hypocrisy.

He didn't open his mouth in retort! He didn't need to!

"Rabbi!" What harm in that? Every Jewish male, from his youth far into manhood, was steeped in the content of the Talmud. If his educational qualifications were acceptable; if in conduct and religious practice he met the required standards; professed credibility with our scriptures and a strict adherence to our law; and was accepted by a substantial number of followers who called him "teacher," he could with much pride claim to be a Rabbi.

It was rumored that Jesus, even as young as twelve years of age had dallied behind in the temple for two days one Passover, to the consternation of his parents, and had absolutely astounded the temple rabbis with his depth of knowledge of Jewish studies.

The problem was that, in this manhood, Jesus had now assumed an authority that he said came directly from his "Father God."

We both knew that such a position was, in the eyes of the Sanhedrin, outright blasphemy, and certainly disqualified him from any identification with the rabbinical school.

In this instant, to use such a title was a term of sarcasm, even though I did not mean it as such.

The first wedge had been driven between any common ground I might have hoped to achieve!

But I continued!

"We know you are a teacher who has come from God."

Then how come we Pharisees had said, "It is only by Beelzebub, the prince of demons, that this fellow drives out demons?"

I couldn't have it both ways. If as a Pharisee I was acknowledging his claim to have come from God, then I was in contradiction with my own profession. I was the hypocrite, not he. To have relegated such an act of love and compassion to demonic influence was consummately despicable! We Pharisees were blasphemous! Not he!

To entertain the thought that Jesus might actually be a prophet sent by God, not to mention his claim to be the Son of God, was to disqualify myself from a lifetime of religious commitment, and my prominent status as a leader of Israel.

The question loomed heavily upon me. Who was on trial here anyway?

But on I babbled!

"For no one could perform the miraculous signs you are doing if God were not with him."

But we had opposed his healing on the Sabbath!

As though God was off duty on the Sabbath! Since when did God choose to do the miraculous on every other day but Saturday?

This seemed to have especially peaked the ire of Jesus beyond the many other man-made rules we Pharisees imposed on the God-seekers.

We did think that he displayed inconsistencies with our Jewish scriptures in his claim that he was the "Lord of the Sabbath."

How could he reconcile such a position when in fact he seemed never to take the Sabbath Day for rest as the Ten Commandments dictated?

Jesus had pointed out a contradiction between our rules and our actions, in that we were never shy of breaking our own rule when it came to salvaging our mule from the ditch should it happen on the Sabbath, for which, no doubt, we had concocted various rules of convenience to "cleanse" us of our indiscretion.

"Is it not lawful to do good on the Sabbath?"

He had us there! Sabbath or no, were we not guilty of, "passing by on the other side," to preserve our dignity, when those who needed our immediate help lay helpless, their condition if not their voice, begging our mercy?

It was more than a parable he had spoken - that incident on the highway when that man fell among thieves. In fact were not all of us guilty of "passing by on the other side," whether personally involved or not, by reason of the callous, yes vicious outcome of our religious rules?

He had given us the bottom line to our discussion. "The Sabbath was made for man, not man for the Sabbath."

He didn't need my compliment! To those in distress Jesus truly was a man who came from God.

For all of our religious pomp, we Pharisees, and in particular the Sanhedrin, were the true Sabbath breakers.

With such an attitude toward the misfortunes of the common people, alas, we could never know to any satisfaction that God was truly with us!

He had not spoken a word, and my first moments with Jesus were strewn in tatters! Now the whole reason for my coming seemed to crumble.

To warn him of impending danger; to seek some common ground; to find some element of defense in the debate with the High Priest? It was all of no consequence now.

The next move was his!

"Yet because I tell the truth, you do not believe me!"

(John 8:45;)

CHAPTER 13

Look Who's Listening

Nicodemus! I cannot say that Jesus used my name verbally when he first spoke, but hear it I did, loud and clear, resonating within the deepest recesses of my soul. It might just as well have been shouted from the rooftops for all to hear, it was so unmistakable. Jesus was not addressing my station, my status; not even my purpose for this visit. He was speaking to me personally!

"(Nicodemus) I tell you the truth, no one can see the kingdom of God unless he is born again."

Here it was! The beginning of the end of my visit! Yet it became a beginning with no ending!

In words to me seemingly incomprehensible, but so pregnant with an unconditional love I had never experienced before, Jesus opened my soul to an inexpressible dawning of light that seemed to have eternal consequence.

Here were words that defied human origin. Here were words that defied every imagination of the mind; that defied every application of logic. Yet, they spoke to the very depths of my soul.

For all my breeding, all my learning, all my religion, I could not find within me any human response that would contribute to the sanctity of this moment.

This visit was no longer a battle for the mind. It was a battle for the soul!

To reward your further interest in my story, I have no recourse but to appeal to your soul. It is there that you will find your treasure when you discover, as I did, that the foundation of a man's existence lies not in reason, but in faith.

"Born again." That got my attention I assure you!

Now, it's your turn! Let him put your name, where he put mine.

"(Your name), I tell you the truth, no one can see the kingdom of God unless he is born again."

Jesus' opening words tossed my whole mind into outer space as it were. Indeed, I was later to discover that he had brought my whole attention to the unseen, yet with more reality than any imagination of my mind could have afforded me.

"Man does not live on bread alone, but on every word that comes from the mouth of God." This philosophy, make that conviction, was a cornerstone of his ministry that he evidently had garnered from that retreat in the desert I mentioned earlier.

This meeting was, by no design of my own, teaching me to "see" with the soul, and not merely with the mind.

True, we have all been moved emotionally beyond reason from time to time. Perhaps it was a good book, or an extraordinary sermon or essay.

To this point in my life I had never been moved so "soulfully" in a manner that would, as it turned out, completely revolutionize my life!

I would enter a phase of life's experience beyond compare with anything I had known hitherto.

It truly was to be as if I had never been born before, and was entering a supremely enriching environment that was beyond compare with what I quite rightly now refer to as my "former life." Only now both lives are conscious realities; not some supposed pre-life existence for which some allege they are now paying penance.

Jesus' next words, "cannot see" had a fullness of meaning that embraced mind and soul. It was comprehension that was compatible with thought processes, but that went beyond an idea (philosophy) to an experience (end result).

So different a life-style would it lead to, that it seemed it could only be expressed as being "born again," as Jesus put it.

Talk about a "knee-jerk" reaction! Indeed I can almost laugh at it; certainly I get a chuckle out of it upon reflection.

"How can a man be born when he is old? Surely he cannot enter a second time into his mother's womb to be born!"

Here was a classic response that illustrates the difference between the two life-styles I have already mentioned; one of religion defined out of philosophy; the other of active relationship based on experience!

Jesus didn't laugh at my question; although did I detect just a hint of twinkle in his eye?

He said in reply "I tell you the truth, no one can enter the kingdom of God unless he is born of water and the Spirit."

His response had no arrogance we all too often associate with those of superior learning. In fact he used my question as an opportunity to assure me it had advanced our discussion to some mutual agreement.

The truth he was advancing was indeed one that was predicated on the human experience. And he was conceding that my baptism with water was a legitimate admittance into the rights of my religion.

This was a human physical ordinance, by some administered at birth, and by others at the point of expressed agreement or conversion to one religion or other, and only that!

He was adding to that the exclusive right of admission to the kingdom of God only by means of the baptism of the Holy Spirit.

He was saying that water baptism sufficed for admission into a religious order, but was not sufficient to permit the soul to enter into a relationship with God, neither in physical or metaphysical terms.

What he had to offer was a God-prepared, a God-chosen, and a God-given baptism into a vital living experiential relationship with our creator.

It was both an entrance into the realm of the Spirit of God and his revolutionary influence upon one's own soul.

This was fellowship far beyond that of religion!

It was fully intended to enrich the minds and hearts of those the Holy Spirit entered, making them enthralled with the God of love who had created them for just such blessings.

I was receiving from Jesus an invitation into a totally new dimension of faith.

But I emphasize it was an invitation, not a coercion! It was mine to accept or to deny.

I was right in one sense. The birth from the womb; physical birth; "born of water" as he put it, was the gateway to a spiritual rebirth of the soul by means of the baptism of the Holy Spirit of God.

He was very careful to differentiate between the two. "Flesh gives birth to flesh," he said, as if of itself it was little more than the creation of just another species. But did not our own scriptures tell us that man was created in the image of God? This was not said of any other creature to be found on the earth.

To be sure, the creation of man was to serve a far higher purpose than the end product of all other created intelligence.

"What was that purpose?" you ask.

Fellowship! Fellowship with my creator! That was my higher purpose in life, far exceeding any other earthly experience I could hope to achieve.

How could I ever achieve such an experience? It was now time to take that leap into the unknown, the untried.

It was time to be "born of the Spirit!"

"...So it is with everyone born of the Spirit."

(John 3:8;)

CHAPTER 14

Do It Right

No, THIS WAS not meant to be another birth! This was to be the concluding act of the birthing process, without which man could not hope to be consummately complete.

If we emphasize the pain of the physical birth process, I now introduce you to the agony of the soul that is identified with being "born of the Spirit."

If we recall the exquisite joy of receiving into our arms the newly born babe that has come out of the natural birthing experience, I now introduce you to an experience that turns one's tears into inexpressible joy. "Joy unspeakable and full of glory" as the old Christian chorus has it. But I am getting ahead of my story!

Jesus anticipated my bewilderment. "You should not be surprised at my saying, 'you must be born again.'"

There were two things I noticed in his statement, the first being the imperative of his comment. "You must!"

It gave me a sense of urgency, as though it were an experience that must not be delayed. It also gave the sense of necessity. This experience was obviously vital to my total life expectancy. But it was a concept far beyond the bounds of my current understanding, something totally new. Eternally conceived. It was something that to date I had never even heard of.

But Jesus was ready for my confusion.

He looked up at the energetic movement of the treetops that accompanied the blustery night of our meeting. This was typical of his teaching style. He was constantly aware of his physical surroundings, and indeed the customs and habits of his enquirers. Repeatedly, as he did now, he wrapped the human experience in the pages of divine truth.

"The wind blows wherever it pleases. You hear its sound, but you cannot tell where it comes from or where it is going."

With this illustration he suggested that all around us are happenings both of limited duration, such as this earthly life; and eternal, as in matters of the soul; that have their own space, yet are played out in our daily lives within the context of a supernatural plan.

All around us, sometimes with, more often without our control, countless orbs of life play out the plan of a supernatural purpose that moves all of life inexorably to predetermined divine objectives. We at best can only live out our life within the confines of our limited understanding, from which point on as Paul later wrote, "we walk by faith, not by sight."

Jesus continued, "So it is with everyone born of the Spirit." Like the wind, the Holy Spirit of God moves upon us. Sometimes he is gentle, almost imperceptible. Other times he moves so quickly that we are overwhelmed with his intent. In either case, he calls us to walk by faith.

Life is turned upside down. The familiar is suddenly blurred. No longer secure, no longer concrete. We are now in unfamiliar territory. The past and present no longer offer security to the mind, much less the soul.

Such was this moment with Jesus! Everything I held to be of importance in my life was on the line!

Strangely, I did not feel threatened. Rather, beyond all question, I sensed that I was somehow once again in a birthing process!

"How can this be?" I asked.

It was his response that really floored me! No, his voice was not harsh. He understood that I was not challenging his teaching. He knew, as did I, that to this point I was just unable to grasp this new concept presented to me.

He responded, "You are Israel's teacher, and do you not understand these things?"

Typical of his debate with us Pharisees, he had answered my question with one of his own.

We both knew full well that the Sanhedrin, and in particular us Pharisees, held our authority in religious and civic matters to be absolute. We had the ancient manuscripts of our heritage at our disposal. All that constitutes the Old Testament of the Christian Bible was the foundation of Jewish faith and tradition. We held the responsibility of its teachings as a sacred trust. But there were two glaring anomalies in our practice.

Since the days of Samuel, the first reformer and founder of the School of the Prophets, our priesthood had maligned every prophet that God had raised up.

Throughout our national history prophet after prophet had forewarned us of impending national disaster at the hands of our enemies, and called the nation to repentance and a return to the faith and practice of the writings of Moses. And time after time our kings and priests alike ignored their message, even to the imprisonment and death of God's messengers.

In precise proportion to our rebellion to the prophetic message, our nation suffered grievous defeat, exile and enslavement at the hands of our enemies.

Even now we were a conquered people.

Secondly, from the banishment from Eden of our first father Adam, God, so we believed, had given promise of a great deliverer who would be raised up to free mankind from sin and uncleanness. He would be born into the Tribe of Judah, and the house of King David, and would sit upon his throne in Jerusalem and rule without end. We called him "Messiah," deliverer.

But since times long past we had despaired of his coming.

Even now here was one among us who had no equal in all of history; who bore the precise ancestry of the Davidic line prophesied; whose every word and act portrayed nothing but hope and love. And here we were, at it again!

We sought to rid ourselves of yet another who posed a threat to our privileged status.

We, who bore the responsibility of preparing the way to final victory, were now the enemies of the very God who could give it to us!

"...We speak of what we know, and we testify to what we have seen,..."

(John 3:11;)

CHAPTER 15

Take It Or Leave It

CLEARLY, THERE WAS no backing down!

If I had come with any thought of rescuing Jesus from impending execution, it had quickly become apparent that I was the one who needed rescuing!

I repeat! In the continuance of our meeting I was being faced with claims and statements the like of which no man had ever before heard nor uttered.

Only after the resolve of the crisis before us would I realize just how enormously privileged I was to have met this Jesus of Nazareth. An experience I trust you already have or will reach in your lifetime.

I did have a choice of course. But my rejection of the claims of Jesus would leave me wallowing in the mire of religious tradition that for centuries had left our nation bereft of any spiritual or political breakthrough.

Yes! I was a teacher of Israel! No! I did not understand these things! Yes! I could accept my ignorance and listen intently to what Jesus was to say next! No! I could turn my back on him and walk away from the very revelation of God that we had waited to hear for more than four hundred years. Yes! I could take the leap of faith that acceptance of his teachings implied. No! I could ignore the offer of those teachings, and in consequence forfeit the glorious revelation of grace that the Law of Moses foreshadowed.

He did not wait for my reply.

"Now listen up!" So his voice implied, if not his words. He assured me that what he had to say was the "honest to God truth," again as the common vernacular has it.

He assured me that what he now had to say, although couched in ethereal terms, had a basis of earthly historic fact. In other words, it was rooted in the prophetic scriptures of our holy book, the Torah!

"I tell you the truth, we speak of what we know, and we testify to what we have seen…"

When he spoke of himself in the plural, I assumed he was aligning himself with the prophets of Israel, all of whom had received the revelation of God through the intervention of the Holy Spirit, and faithfully recorded the heavenly message received for our enlightenment.

What he was saying could be corroborated by the prophetic and historic books of our scriptures, and our impeccable national genealogical records, if we chose to examine them.

I have already stated in earlier paragraphs our grievous sins perpetrated against those very prophets. And now Jesus! Either we, (make that I), could choose to believe what I professed to represent, or I could share in the perpetrating of the most heinous crime ever committed in all of history.

All I had to do was trace the genealogy of Jesus; compare his words and actions with prophetic scripture; examine the witness of those who had been involved at his birth, and accept the testimonies of the thousands who had been the recipients of his miracles; and I would have the perfect match.

Had not all of them told their stories repeatedly to whoever would listen?

Had not King Herod perpetrated the slaughter of the innocents just thirty or so years before in the hope of obliterating any pretence to his throne?

Had not the humble shepherds of Bethlehem joyously shouted their praises of the babe they had found in a manger in Bethlehem?

Had not some Kings from the Far East traveled extensively in response to astrological signs that heralded the birth of a divinely appointed king?

Mind you! All of this had taken place within my lifetime! And in some sense, as a leader in Israel, I was party to the whole event. No wonder Jesus could rightly accuse me, in the first person, of not accepting his testimony.

"I have spoken to you of earthly things and you do not believe; how then will you believe if I speak of heavenly things."

My rejection of these earthly claims could only prove detrimental to my grasp of the spiritual claims he was about to make. It would soon become apparent that his implications were as far reaching, as they were controversial.

But it was his next statement that really threw me!

"No one has ever gone into heaven except the one who came from heaven – the Son of Man."

He was claiming to have existed in Heaven before his earthly existence, and was properly divine in nature. To my mind this implied that before I sat in his presence, he had free access to both heaven and earth as required.

Now don't quit reading here! I know how you might feel at this point, because rejection of his claim was certainly my first reaction.

But I knew my scriptures well enough to remember that Father Abraham had given tithes to Melchizedek, king of Salem, who was called, "Priest of God Most High," a person of no known ancestry prior to nor after his encounter with Abraham.

King David the Psalmist had identified this priest with our expected Messiah, defining him as having no beginning and no ending.

What's more, angels visited Abraham from heaven, pronouncing the birth of his son Isaac by means of Sarah, his wife.

Clearly, it was not for me to give credit to our Holy Scriptures in one case, and deny any supposition that there was free, and likely frequent, sorties between Heaven and Earth.

But to accept as truth Jesus' statement, was to acknowledge that our long-awaited Messiah had at last come to us, for surely we expected no less a person than one who had the true anointing of God upon him.

And though we acknowledge there were many messianic pretenders throughout our years of bondage, "Never a man spoke as did this man;" so acknowledged some soldiers we had earlier sent to arrest him; an assignment they aborted.

Furthermore, their tenure was bent on armed uprising against our enemies, each in turn defeated, to suffer indescribable suffering and death.

In marked contrast, Jesus came in peace with a love and compassion for our nation that was indisputably demonstrated by his teachings, verified by his miraculous healings of the sick, and even the raising of the dead.

So! Did I believe him to be the promised Messiah? Well my friend, that was to depend on the coming of the, "Wind," as much for you as it was for me!

CHAPTER 16

The Teacher

To this point I had not introduced the true purpose of my meeting with Jesus. But, as you may have already guessed, he had set the agenda long before I arrived.

Indeed, I was later to realize that the next phase of our conversation had been set in Heaven, even before I was born, even before Jesus was born to this earth; in short, as the Scriptures state, "Before the foundation of the world."

I could sense a change in the aura of our meeting.

There had been no threatening challenge to my status, or my theology. Even the issue of his obvious power with God did not belittle my ego. Rather, his next words came in tones of love and compassion the like of which I had never heard before.

A father might scold a child for wrongs committed, but he would cradle them in his arms and explain to them his reasons for his actions and encourage them to do better.

The relationship mended, he might read them a story, or help them with their homework, or to solve a problem.

Just so, he had long anticipated my purpose and had quickly put to rest the antagonisms and contradictions of the religious confrontations I represented, in deference to the needs of my soul.

I was about to hear the greatest story of love ever told!

Me! Alone with Jesus! Taught by the very one who would unswervingly be true to his convictions; who would pay whatever price required in fulfillment of the destiny he believed he was born for.

I knew instinctively that I was privileged beyond all deserving to be in company with the greatest soul of human kind that ever had existed. I was as close to God in that moment as ever a man could be.

The voice was human, but his purpose was divine! Every word he spoke was drenched in the full realization of what they meant to his God and to each unflinching step he was about to walk in the greatest journey a human being could ever undertake.

Each anticipated step would overflow with love for his fellow men, no matter their pro or con of his claims, no matter the vehemence of their rejection.

Whatever their reaction, what he was about to reveal to me would stand eternally before the God of Heaven as the measure of guilt or innocence of all human kind from Adam to the last soul at the bar of judgment.

That included *me*! That includes *you*!

There it was again! What would I do with Jesus? The question continued to confront me. There was no way around it. Ignore it, rationalize it, or reject it. Until I acted upon it, it would never go away.

His next words took me back in Jewish history to the wilderness journey of the Israelites at a place infested with venomous snakes, used by God to turn their rebellious hearts back to him.

Moses was instructed to make an image of a snake upon a pole and raise it up in full view of the people. To this point many people had died from the snakebites, but now all others bitten could look to the erected pole and would be saved from certain death.

Jesus continued.

"Just as Moses lifted up the snake in the desert, so the Son of Man must be lifted up…"

One would think that their liberation from slavery would have made them the most grateful people on the face of the earth. But the old feud of centuries past between Jacob and Esau erupted once more as the Israelites were denied permission to pass through Edom, Esau territory, to complete an exodus from Egypt that would have taken only a few short weeks instead of forty years.

The age-old conflict between human will verses divine will was quick to surface, and the people were determined that God would do it their way, or not at all. Of course poor Moses again took the brunt of their stubbornness.

Now I don't want you to think that my tale has turned into a sermon. Jesus' inclusion of this ancient history was vital to my understanding of what he was about to teach me.

Because us human beings are bedewed with free will and choice, he wanted me to realize the affinity of obedience with my wellbeing.

I was all too familiar with the extraordinary deficiencies of our religious practices, perpetrated by centuries of repeated rebellion, idolatry and consequent subjection to our enemies, as we were even now to our Roman conquerors.

By inference, he was leading me to see the utter hopelessness of our religious, political, social, or even personal determination to bring peace to the human soul. He wanted me to understand that the sense of our innate hunger for the source, purpose and meaning of life was God-driven. We did not make God. He made us.

We did not presume upon him. We were to submit to him. The predicament of life itself requires the resolve of divine intervention into the human psyche, body, mind and spirit.

He understood completely that, like no other nation on earth, throughout history, Israel had been chosen by God as the race through whom God would resolve the sin issue that afflicted all mankind. He had stated before that he had not come to destroy the law that we believed came directly from God through Moses, but rather to fulfill it.

Despite the repeated backslidings of our nation, God's chosen Messiah would, in human terms, be a Jew. Wasn't it high time we stopped killing every prophet that came along and sincerely examine the credentials of every pretender to this divine position? If so we would clearly see that Jesus indisputably fulfilled in lineage, and in prophecy, the credentials of our long awaited Messiah, not to mention the overwhelming benevolence of his teaching and miraculous signs.

It was the extension of this teaching into the personal realm that was to bring to all sincere seekers the final peace of mind and heart that would settle the God question for all eternity, *without the trappings of religious ceremony.*

But why a snake, you ask? Could there be a grosser object to look upon with any expectation of healing? Was not the serpent the tool of Satan in the Garden of Eden when all this sin business began? Why the snake?

Clearly the imagery of the snake was in reference to original sin, when Satan, disguised as a serpent, had lured Adam and Eve into disobedience to God's command.

There in that desert, for the person bitten to look upon that snake was to personally admit that they had sinned against God, and deserved to die. But in so looking, they would live, forgiven for their transgression.

Did the pole represent a cross, like the preferred weapon of execution of the Roman regime?

How exceedingly convenient, that we religious potentates could put the blame for such a hideous murder on the shoulders of an indifferent Roman conqueror!

A snake? What gives?

That was supreme, unconditional love we were about to nail up there! That was an absolutely pure and undefiled sacrificial lamb we were about to drive those spikes into!

Then it hit me like an unexpected missile!

Could it be possible that we were about to crucify, in the person of Jesus, the very atonement for our sins we would celebrate in our temple in just a few days time at our Passover Celebrations?

Would not the innocent unblemished lamb used in our ceremony become the bearer of our sin? Was not its blood expected to atone for our sins for at least another year?

Could it be that Jesus saw himself as such an atonement for all the sins of man throughout all time, past, present and future?

Oh unspeakable horror! He was about to sacrifice himself to become sin for us! Snake indeed! At least until the blood flowed!

"For God so loved the world that he gave his one and only Son,..."

(John 3:16;)

CHAPTER 17

Who's Who

BUT THERE WAS more.

"...that everyone who believes in him may have eternal life."

Whoa! Did I just hear what I thought I heard?

Was he actually expecting people, or for that matter me in particular, to believe that this willful suicidal act would achieve for us reconciliation with God for all eternity?

Why would he do something like that? Did he think that by sacrificing himself he could actually obtain the salvation of his own soul, let alone our nation, and much less the whole world? Surely no man alive or dead could single-handedly appease a God who had obliterated all human kind for their transgressions, save for Noah and family. He would have to be a god himself to do that!

Bingo!!!

Oh! Surely not! Surely he didn't claim to be that! A God, or perhaps even actually God our creator? But there was just no place left to go in our discussion.

We had covered the proverbial bases. First base: The desperate squalid deprivation of human kind had no remedy outside of the soul issue. Second base: Religion had miserably failed to save us by reason of its human sin-ridden contamination. Third base:

Every prophet recorded in our history had been denied access to our hearts and minds. There was simply nowhere left to turn, no other remedy short of the intervention of Almighty God himself.

And now there it lay outstretched before us the quantum leap to home plate. If Jesus wasn't God, then it didn't much matter who he was. Only God could save us now!

If he was a debater, he had won hands down. He had me cornered because he had turned every one of my potential arguments into pulp before I could even formulate them in my mind. But this was no contest of the mind. This was undeniably a contest of the heart.

If he had stopped right there; If he had laid out his thesis as a take-it-or-leave-it proposition, I admit he would have lost me right then and there, as indeed was the case for the majority of his audiences over the past three years of his short ministry. Even a band of seventy-six disciples had by this time dwindled to twelve, and he was soon to lose one more, if not all of them.

With my theological training, and my devout defense of our religion, there remained, to my mind, no rationale for accepting prima-facie any justification for his impending action.

But there is yet one other reference that begs our attention concerning the title he had just used in reference to himself: "The Son of Man."

That I've acknowledged his conviction that divine involvement underscored his determined sacrifice, I concede. But there was absolutely no doubt in my mind that I was addressing a full-blooded human being. He was truly and properly "man."

I think this fact was of great concern to him because he had throughout his ministry repeatedly used the same reference to himself as "The Son of Man."

And if his impending crucifixion was to be the martyrdom of yet another zealot, and there had been a number, then the best he could hope for was his name added to the list of national heroes who laid down their lives for our cause. But it wouldn't change anything.

Why would he then claim that if we would believe in him we would be granted eternal life? There surely was a greater expectation of himself that he felt was justified, beyond the accolades of a war memorial.

And there was!

But even this claim would not compromise his true humility. He shifted my attention from himself with one deft statement that forever has etched itself indelibly into the annals of history.

"For God so loved the world that he gave his one and only Son, that whoever believes in him shall not perish but have eternal life."

He would have to be a god himself to do that! Isn't that what I have just written above?

And now there it lay outstretched before us, the quantum leap to home plate."

I repeat myself. But that's the issue that remains for all mankind throughout all ages, as it did for me.

The playing field had now leveled out. There was no sense that Jesus was claiming to be the originator of the plan of redemption he championed. God was!

Had he not made numerous references to God as his father? Indeed he had even suggested that the intimacy of that relationship was like that of the little child who calls out to his father, "Abba" – "Daddy." And we Jews considered it blasphemy to even mention the name of our God, "Yahweh." Such references had been a perpetual thorn in the side of us Pharisees. How could any human being be so flippant in reference to their God?

That was the problem!

We had made God so remote from our earthly concerns that he had scarcely any credibility among the general populace, including us for that matter.

Now Jesus was ranking himself as the Son of God! But mark this well! It was a relationship that he conferred upon all his converts. And his disciples lost no time in embracing that relationship.

John, who had brought me to this meeting with Jesus would later write, "How great is the love the Father has lavished on us, that we should be called children of God! And that is what we are!"

The exception being, that Jesus was inferring that he existed with God before he had been born into this world. Not only so, but that he was the "one and only Son."

This was the foundation of his justification, yes, even imperative for the sacrifice he was about to make.

Now mark this! We Jews have never had any compunction about our reference to the Spirit of God in what we have accepted as the divine works of God. By inference we concede that the existence of that Spirit bears the same affinity as the existence of God – no beginning and no end! Are we then to relegate Jesus to a second thought in the eternal purposes of God?

No! He made no other inference but that, as God had always existed, so had he. "…Father, Son and Holy Ghost, undivided in essence and co-equal in power and glory." So one of the Christian Churches was later to state in its doctrinal thesis.

We were now half way down the final base line to home plate. To stop now to question the coach who had signaled us to round the bases would mean utter disaster.

If it was "the Son of God" we were to nail to the cross, and to be sure it was really us, and not the Romans that would do this, it was for the very least, *the heart of God who would hang there.*

What a God! What love! What sacrifice! What sin! What deliverance!

Outrageous! So is heard the cry of logic. "What red-blooded, intelligent son of anyone, much less God, would even consent to such a demand from his father"?

But how quickly we forget!

One of our favorite stories about Abraham was his obedience to God to offer up Isaac his son as a sacrifice as proof of his allegiance. But what of the son, who thought his father must have forgotten to tether the sacrifice to the entourage, and looked endlessly for it as they traveled to the appointed site? "God himself will provide a lamb for the offering, my son." So assured Abraham.

No word of protest from Isaac is recorded as his father bound him hand and foot and laid him on the altar, although common sense would suggest a struggle and bolt to freedom, easily outrunning his near century old father.

Clearly, Abraham's obedience to God was not the sole object of the story. The obedience of the son looms large in God's strategy. And the obedience of both father and son was rewarded with the ram caught in the thicket, prophetic of the impending sacrifice Jesus was to make on the cross.

But now, so it seemed, it was God's turn!

From the teenage enthusiasm of young Isaiah through the ranks of succeeding prophets, the responsive cry to God's loving heart was "Here am I Lord, send me." But that cry had not been heard in Israel for over four centuries.

Was God one final time asking "Whom shall I send? And who will go for us?" If so, it was quite evident Jesus had already said in his heart, "Here am I Lord, send me."

Only this time there would be no lamb in the thicket!!!

"...Light has come into the world,..."

(John 3:19;)

CHAPTER 18

Not So Fast

You PERHAPS CAN imagine the overwhelming turmoil of my emotions as I sat there and received, for the first time ever uttered, words of longed-for hope. Utterly bereft of spiritual insight, beyond the Torah and subsequent religious rites, I was given a mental and spiritual jolt beyond the ecstasy of any highpoint I had ever experienced in my pursuit of spiritual peace.

For those of you, long grounded in your God relationship, this must beg the question, "Did you come to faith in Jesus at that meeting?"

For those of you still confronted with your conclusions about Jesus, there is likely more sympathy for my dilemma.

For myself, even now I cannot say with certainty that this meeting with Jesus swayed my heart and mind right there and then. But I will concede, as I have before intimated, it had started a process that would ultimately change my life forever and eternity.

Neither did Jesus belabor the points he had made. Instead, he now undertook to address the conflict with the Sanhedrin that had arisen over the course of his ministry.

There was no trace of the former vehemence he had displayed in earlier confrontations with the Sanhedrin. In fact he did not raise any of the issues those meetings had divulged. Nor did he give opportunity for me to renew my initial plan to address my forebodings about his probable arrest.

Instead, he wanted me to see that his coming on the scene, his subsequent ministry, and his impending sacrifice were the predetermined decisions of a loving God.

"For God did not send his Son into the world to condemn the world, but to save the world through him."

Though these words were meant for all people, to my mind it was saying loud and clear, the torment of my own soul was not to be exacerbated by a perpetually nagging conscience. Nor was his conflict with the Sanhedrin the real issue. He had come in peace at the behest of a truly loving God who had determined that the darkness of sin that alienated us from his fellowship could, and would, be appeased through faith in his Son.

It was as though God was asking, "What more can I do for your eternal salvation than to give up my only begotten Son for the propitiation of your sin?" And it was as obvious as it was essential that our only hope, make that our last hope was to believe in Jesus as the literal savior of our soul.

Conclusion! The choice was ours!

If we believed he was the Son of God, sent to redeem us, we could at last find rest for our soul. Reject Jesus and there was no fresh condemnation; we already stood steeped in it, and we could wait for the end of time, try any other remedy we might think useful, serve God with the most elaborate religious rhetoric possible for the rest of our lives, and still find we were lost in our sins.

The words of one of Jesus' earlier teachings came immediately to mind.

"Not everyone who says to me, 'Lord, Lord, will enter the kingdom of heaven, but only he who does the will of my Father who is in heaven."

He went on to emphasize that many false prophets would arise to deceive many, turning them from faith to good works and religious exercise. But only those who by simple faith in him obeyed in their conscience the Spirit's prompting would ultimately find eternal life. In other words, a successful relationship with a holy omnipotent God rested solely on faith in his Son Jesus Christ who would guide their heart and mind into all truth.

Next, he made his demand airtight by discounting our supposed ignorance of our sins. You see, we Jews had been steeped in the keeping of the Law of Moses, contained in our Torah. Its multiple religious rites and rules for living a life pleasing to God had brought to us the disciplines of a godly life, but did not provide us with any measure by which we could declare ourselves acceptable to God, much less our conscience.

This dilemma was further complicated by the Talmud, our book of regulations that laid down procedures supposedly designed to make it possible for us to keep the law successfully. But we all knew that such a goal, as worthy as that might be, was impossible to attain, a point that Jesus was frequent to make in his teachings to the common people.

To repeat myself, he took no issue with the Torah, but he was livid in his outright condemnation of the Talmud, because he found therein deliberate misrepresentations of the law, obviously designed, for the very least, to convenience the religious leaders in their personal application of the law; and worse, to condemn the masses for whom there was no possible way to adhere to the requirements of their teachers.

The end result was a massive detachment of the common people from any hope or even interest in religious exercise, much less a personal savior.

But now, through Jesus, "…Light has come into the world…"

There was no further excuse, be it through the misapplication of the Law; or be it a personal rejection of the Son of God, Jesus, the Messiah for whom we had waited so many centuries.

Furthermore, he claimed such denial was precipitated by blatant sin that, despite its clandestine nature, was thoroughly known to God.

"…but men loved darkness instead of light because their deeds were evil."

Now this statement was of supreme importance! It came as the nail in the coffin of our false righteousness.

Jesus exposed the inherent sinful nature of man, precipitated by the fall from grace of our first parents, Adam and Eve.

"Everyone who does evil hates the light, and will not come into the light for fear that his deeds will be exposed. But whoever lives by the truth comes into the light, so that it may be seen plainly that what he has done has been done through God."

His statement, in my opinion, had far more subtlety than first we comprehend.

Why the greater haste to confirm our good deeds, than to confess the admission of our misdeeds?

Now, I am sure he was not placing a taboo upon any accolade earned by doing the right. But in context he was saying that works of righteousness were of themselves insufficient to redeem the soul, because they did not prevent further sinning. Rather, they tended to highlight the deprivation of the soul that could bless and curse almost in the same breath.

Sometime after the Jerusalem believers in Jesus had established the Christian religion, James, the earthly brother of Jesus and Bishop of Jerusalem would write, "With the tongue we praise our Lord and Father, and with it we curse men, who have been made in God's likeness. Out of the mouth come praise and cursing. My brothers, this should not be."

Where then was the cure?

To be sure the cure did not exist with the human heart. But Jesus had declared that anyone who would believe in him as God's anointed Son, God's chosen Messiah, would live in such a light of truth and understanding that, despite the limitations of their earthly existence, they would produce a manifestation of such love and grace, deeds and words as, without contradiction, could only have come to them from God himself.

The wind blew across our path again, as though to say, "come follow me. I know from whence I have come and wither I go."

My meeting with Jesus was at an end!

"…It would be better for him if he had not been born."

(Matthew 26:24;)

CHAPTER 19

Judas

T HE NIGHT WAS well spent and dawn was just breaking on the horizon when Jesus summoned Peter and John who were ever near at hand in these perilous times. He was sending them into Jerusalem to arrange the place where he and his disciples would observe the Passover. It would be no trouble for them to conduct me off their hidden trail to the main road where Joseph of Arimathea would join me for my unobtrusive return to Jerusalem.

It was while we were on the trail that Peter and John abruptly pulled me off the path into a thicket, seconds before another disciple, Judas Iscariot, passed our position, hastily headed for the city. He was alone. We went unnoticed. None of us could have guessed his intent.

Arriving at home, I was greeted by my wife, who aware of my departure offered no question as to why I had been so long gone from the house. She simply prepared me a good breakfast during which we were joined by some of our younger children still bleary-eyed from sleep that I had been denied, and totally unaware of my absence.

It was almost time to leave for the Temple for the usual meeting of the Sanhedrin. Did I say "usual?" It would be a meeting I would never forget, made the more clandestine by the presence of Jesus amid the doting crowd in another porch of the Temple where the common people heard him gladly.

There was a decided air of excitement among the members present. Annas, the High Priest seemed much more, how do you say it – "up beat?" Certainly he wasn't his usual pompous self, (honestly garnered from years of solicitude from the least to the greatest of Israel). In fact I thought he seemed almost congenial and himself solicitous toward us members.

It was obvious that something was up!

Then he announced it! Speaking for the Acting High Priest, (Caiaphas seldom addressed the assembly in deference to his high office). Annas announced that there had come to them earlier this morning one of Jesus' disciples who sought to betray him.

He was, in fact, the treasurer of their group, and sought, as he put it, "some compensation for the other disciples," in return for leading us to Jesus. But we knew that such a blatant lie served only to sooth his conscience.

It was rumored that he regularly absconded group funds for his own personal purposes.

Judas Iscariot was his name. It seemed riches was his game.

Why?

This was a very important question, given that he had been hand picked by Jesus, as had all of the twelve disciples that still remained with him.

He had traveled with the group for all three years of Jesus' ministry. He had sat at the feet of one who was already ranked as surely the greatest teacher of all time, certainly among the greats of our impressive religious history.

This act of betrayal was certainly strange, given that he had been one of the twelve disciples who Jesus had actually sent on a preaching mission with the power to heal the sick, raise the dead and cast out demons. We know that they were successful because of the testimonies of the recipients of their ministry, not to mention their elation at the success they had experienced.

How then could this man Judas possibly have walked away from power and grace like that?

Oh yes! To be sure the vast majority of the Sanhedrin cajoled that "every man has his price." "Money talks." But not all of us were that vocal. There were some expressions of incredulity in the room, and even some very heavy hearts, mine among them.

Did I detect the slightest hint of a tear in the eyes of Joseph of Arimathea? Was the silence of Gamaliel an indication of his utter disgust at this turn of events? He was certainly one to express caution when we were prone to give way to hasty decisions.

Beyond the obvious delight of Annas, and some pretentious abash on the face of Caiaphas, and the usual plaudits of those in the seats of greater honor, there seemed to me to be a strange uneasiness among the majority of members.

Mind you, there was no debating the question, so to speak. The hierarchy had already agreed upon, and paid Judas, the sum of thirty silver coins, ironically the price of the least marketable slave.

He would advise our appointed liaison at first opportunity of the time and place we could arrest Jesus unobtrusively, as to do so publicly would most certainly create a riot among the crowds present for the Passover.

As for the disciples, our contingent was organized, large enough to overcome their anticipated violent protection of their Lord. This included a goodly number of the Roman Guard that was at the disposal of the High Priest.

It was to be understood that the only involvement of Judas would be to identify Jesus to the arresting officers, a selection of soldiers determined by the Centurion of the guard to have had no earlier official or casual contact with Jesus.

It was the method of identification of Jesus that would be used by Judas that confounded Jew and Roman alike. Why not just use the pointed finger? Why not just have some of the soldiers grab him while the others deterred the disciples?

No! It was to be a kiss!

It was then that the meeting took a most sinister turn. What would the Sanhedrin do with Jesus?

We all knew what was coming next. The vote on any decision would be a mockery, because Caiaphas had already addressed the question in a meeting that had followed the raising from the dead of Lazarus, brother to Mary and Martha of Bethany who hosted Jesus and his disciples whenever they were in town. That event had brought the problem to a head.

There seemed to be no way of stopping him. To be sure this miracle had swayed many Jews to believe in him as their Messiah. There was no telling what future mega healings or resurrections from the dead might take place, removing any options of intervention the Sanhedrin might entertain.

Our concern was two-fold.

If the people, by overwhelming odds were to make Jesus King of Israel, then the Romans would at least arrest all of us, including the High Priest, and in all probability would execute us, including Jesus, and assume supreme authority over the nation and suppress completely any formal expression of our religion.

"You know nothing at all!"

The bitter sarcasm of the raised voice of Caiaphas broke into the buzz of meanderings we members raised throughout the room. We got the message! We useless puppets of our religious hierarchy were to be made complicit to the self-serving whim of the supreme potentate of our nation. And it isn't the other puppet, King Herod' I'm talking about.

Caiaphas was out to save his own skin. There was no finger pointing either! Each member of the Sanhedrin was in exactly the same position.

"You do not realize that it is better for you that one man die for the people than that the whole nation perish," he continued.

What logic! What obvious justification for such a dastardly act!

But it was the kind of execution that Caiaphas wanted that created a problem.

We Jews did not have the authority to crucify any citizen. Such executions were exclusively subject to the whims of our Roman conquerors.

But such a rule provided a hidden motive for our sinister decision. By laying blame on Caesar, public qualms could easily be abated.

But all was not cut and dried.

How were we to change his popularity with the people into a demand for crucifixion? It was one thing to convince Pilate that Jesus was worthy of death. Even if he somehow agreed with us, he would surely be restrained by the vociferous adulations of the people.

For a bribe the remedy could be found in the planting of our agents throughout the crowd they would recruit from the rabble population, ready for whatever turn-of-events we might encounter. Any pro Jesus sympathizers in attendance would be very few, and their protests well drowned out, since the trial would not be posted publicly and would presumably be held in the wee hours of the morning, well before the general public were aroused from their sleep. Any instructions required could be circulated quite quickly throughout the rabble ranks, raising a din in favor of whatever results we deemed necessary.

We were all aware of the annual custom of Pilate to release a prisoner, chosen by the people at the celebration of Passover, as a solicitous act of recognition of this most holy day in the Jewish calendar.

The prime candidate for this fortuitous act was clearly Barabbas. Although an insurrectionist against Rome, and a murderer to boot, his release would be the epitome of flattery to Pilate that he should be so condescending. It would present no difficulty in persuading the crowd to demand the release of one who had laid his life on the line for Jewish emancipation.

Given the threat to our national security, and the threat to our personal prestige, and given that the plot was in place, (and I'll let you decide our priority in that list), there was no doubt that the High Priest would receive our unanimous vote in favor of his plan.

As if we were in control!

As the disciple John was later to write in his gospel concerning the advice of Caiaphas, "He did not say this on his own, but as high priest that year he prophesied that Jesus would die for the Jewish nation, and not only for that nation but also for the scattered children of God, to bring them together and make them one. So from that day on they plotted to take his life."

We did not grasp at the time, even though confirmed by the very history of our nation, that God had always maintained control of our destiny, and even now his will was being worked out in the final fulfillment of the Jewish law and prophets, in the coming of Jesus Christ as Lord and Savior of all mankind.

But if prophecy from God had been uttered from the lips of our High Priest, the glory of its utterance would soon be decimated by the blasphemous incrimination Caiaphas would soon bring upon the people over whom he presided!

The meeting concluded with the instruction that we should be ready to reassemble at a moments notice, as the arrest was to take place this very night, and the matter disposed of before morning light, to avoid any violation of Passover.

"Here I am! I stand at the door and knock..."

(Rev. 3:20;)

CHAPTER 20

No Turning Back

IF I HAD any thought of laying aside contemplation of those hours with Jesus for a more convenient time, I was mistaken.

To begin with, the intellectual battle with my heritage versus the teachings of Jesus was quickly acquiescing to an emotional battle with conscience. No matter the rationale or lack of it, the question loomed larger than ever. "What will I do with Jesus?"

No man could have been more greatly favored than I. To have heard from his own lips the revelation of his claim to be my personal redeemer. To have been the first non-disciple to confront his claims to be the fulfillment of our Messianic hope of national deliverance. To have personally witnessed such love and commitment as to offer himself up to the indescribable suffering of a cross for the salvation of his nation. To be personally taught a new and different resolve for sin and uncleanness of which our Mosaic Law was supposedly the forerunner. To be standing on the brink of an historic breakthrough when that law would achieve its divine purpose through the fulfillment of its prophecies.

I could never have guessed that all of my heritage, all of my education, all of my success in life, my very position in the Sanhedrin would bring me to the greatest challenge of my life.

Faith!

There was no backing down! Either I believed him, or I didn't. And if I did, then I would have to stand in the breach before the Sanhedrin and risk the loss of everything I had striven so successfully to achieve.

Though I did not realize it then, I was now engaged in the very personal battle for the salvation of my very soul. The battle that had its beginning before the very foundation of creation. The battle that would achieve its victory on a cross!

There surely could have been no soul on earth in more misery than I as we each left the room to grapple with our own private thoughts.

Oh, it had been a long time coming. A whole three years of struggle with an itinerant roaming preacher that had set a whole nation on edge. And now the plot was in motion. Surely the dastardly act could not be stopped. There loomed only one last hope. Someone was going to have to stand in his defense. But at what a price!

No, I don't change the subject by bringing my wife into my story.

Jewish women were by tradition the silent heroes of our nation, although there were some who achieved national acclaim. Deborah and Queen Esther come to mind. The first ruled as a Judge of Israel before the establishment of a king. And Esther, though, or even because she was the wife of the King of Persia, saved our nation from certain extinction.

Such aside, it is fair to say that Jewish women, for all their privacy, exerted much influence in the fabric of our national society. I suppose it is true of all society; the hand that rocks the cradle rules the nation.

My wife was no exception.

I was always able to trust her with my innermost thoughts. Ours had been a very stable marriage, our family life exemplary, the more thanks to her than to her prestigious husband.

She read me like a book; a fact most men are reluctant to admit. She certainly knew I was more upset than she had seen me for a long time, perhaps ever. Still she had said nothing, biding her time, waiting for the moment when I would most certainly bring her into the inner sanctum of my heart.

Mind you, this time the subject matter was to be far different to the usual political and social malaise of the day. But she already knew what it would be!

I was always careful to avoid names, unless of course they were a positive influence in resolve of my concerns. But the central focus of our discussion was to be probably the most mentioned name in all of Jerusalem at the time. Jesus!

I told her where I had been overnight. She showed no hint of surprise. I shared the purpose of my meeting and I divulged the content of my conversation with Jesus, or more to the point his commentary, for he was the teacher. I was the student.

She showed neither concern nor delight, but her demeanor portrayed an instant interest in what I had to tell her, and I knew she was of one heart with me in my spirit, and would be understanding of my dilemma.

After all, she and our family, and not a few of our many relatives stood to be victims of gossip and disrepute, dependant upon my potential action.

Surprising calmness pervaded our conversation, even when we discussed such possible consequences as my banishment from the Sanhedrin, with the real threat of shunning by my religious, political and business colleagues. And any of these were conceivably the lesser consequences that may well be overshadowed by arrest and charges of treason.

We were a conquered nation under the whims of an indifferent regime, who at any excuse would eliminate any pretense to the ruling of our own affairs.

King Herod was our monarch by rightful succession, but his present jurisdiction was confined to the province of Galilee, and to the religious overtones of our daily life.

Rome was only too happy to concede to us control of such "fanatical" expressions of religious interests.

Certainly, my wife and I had never confronted so serious a dilemma as this one in all our married life. And what of our children, both at home and those who were married and raising their own families?

But her reaction was not as I had expected. Indeed, did I detect a faint smile?

"Nicodemus, my beloved husband, I too am a believer in Jesus!"

The silence that pursued was too sacred to be "deafening," as the common vernacular has it! There seemed to be a sweet overwhelming spirit in the room, much as two hearts confirm what cannot be spoken. But this was somehow different to human emotion. Yes, it was singly in the heart of each of us. But it was also all around us, filling the room with an essence indefinable by any human senses.

Certainly, we had never known this moment before now.

My heart knew only a sense of relief that not only now did she know of my predicament, she understood, because she also had reached a personal conclusion that Jesus was indeed our promised Messiah.

But I was also troubled because she had made her confession inclusive of us both. "Too." "Also." "With." However defined, she was telling me that she was aware that I believed in Jesus, when to this moment I was still struggling with the thought.

"Now hold on a minute! Let's not be too hasty! There is a lot to figure out here!" Those thoughts were on my lips but as yet unspoken.

We both knew there was great risk in such a decision, because such a confession now precipitated the much-feared action I was about to take.

I would go to his defense. At his trial I would expose my sympathies for this beleaguered soul and bring down upon my head only God himself knew what!

But that was the problem.

I had gone to him to more clearly understand him, to warn him of impending danger, to find some way of reconciliation that would appease him and the Sanhedrin.

Then he was just a man. Now, if I truly believed what my wife had sensed in my heart, he was now my Savior!

Still, the battle continued. Which will it be: the coveting of my worldly benefits, or my acquiescence to the healing of my soul?

It was a spiritual struggle completely foreign to the worldly mind, utterly irrational and a threat to one's well being as we understood it. Still, it spoke to that indefinable, yet persistent aching void of the heart that all the wealth and success of this life could not quench.

Only God knew the depth of my struggle. And next to him there stood my wife in agony of heart for the man she loved as, ready or not, he stood at the portal awaiting the knock that would thrust him into the blackest night this world has ever known.

"...Yet not my will, but yours be done."

(Luke 22:42;)

CHAPTER 21

Battle Lines

E<small>VEN AS MY</small> wife and I commiserated on the impending fate of Jesus and our own future, the dastardly act was underway.

I must first explain that I do not tell this part of my story from personal observance. But I do write with sufficient confidence that the facts, as I present them, are substantially accurate, given my position in the Sanhedrin.

I do know that the accounts of Jesus' arrest that were later to be written could easily differ in some details, given the mass confusion that always accompanies any such event.

I've already mentioned the rabble crowd that by now would be assembling at the Governor's residence, and some chosen to witness against Jesus, would be waiting at the home of Annas the Chief Priest emeritus.

Of course Judas Iscariot led the arresting party to the secluded grove where Jesus, his disciples and their entourage were encamped. The arresting party consisted of a detachment of the Temple Guard, a garrison that was assigned for the protection of life and property of the Jewish religious leaders and the Temple complex. There were added to the troops a number of the rabble crowd to assure overwhelming numbers to that of Jesus' group.

I am most grateful to the Apostle John who later shared with me some most sacred details of that night on the Mount of Olives.

Though I was not there of course, I include his account here because those moments at Gethsemane are absolutely critical to an understanding of all that followed.

I leave the account of the intimate Passover supper shared between Jesus and his disciples to John's own personal Gospel that bears his name. Suffice to say that Jesus used the occasion to expose the traitor among them. Even before the supper was concluded Jesus sent Judas from their midst instructing him to get the dastardly deed done quickly.

John told of the somber atmosphere that pervaded that band of the now eleven disciples as their Lord led them back to their encampment.

As he continued with the accounts of that night, I could surmise something of the agony of soul that must have pervaded that little band of men that had shared the constant fellowship of Jesus for three years. I was not prepared for the excruciating detail of the intimate pathos of Jesus as he spent his last night on this earth.

It is left to one's imagination the profundity of the shock and disbelief; the anger and disappointment; the despair that must have permeated the band of followers in the lower camp when the disciples shared the events of that evening.

But it was to be only Peter, James and John who would witness the unprecedented conflict their Lord and Master was to endure that night.

Jesus had not entered the lower camp, but rather, he went straight to his private grove. He had asked the three to accompany him to this place of prayer, while the remaining eight he had sent to tell and console the others in the lower encampment.

As they entered the smaller grove next to his place of prayer, Jesus confided that his very soul was so overwhelmed with sorrow that his heart could have burst from the shear agony.

Wouldn't that have saved his enemies from the guilt of their proposed bloody plot?

Jesus asked the three of them to keep watch over him while he went to the rock of prayer where he had spent so very many hours in communion with his Heavenly Father.

John was chagrinned to admit that despite their best intentions, the overwhelming events of that day had completely exhausted them, and when Jesus came away from his first session of prayer he found all three of them sound asleep.

Now, they most certainly had been the objects of rebuke on numerous occasions throughout those years of discipleship. But it was plain to hear the hurt in Jesus' voice when he asked Peter, "Could you men not keep watch with me for one hour? Watch and pray so that you will not fall into temptation. The spirit is willing, but the body is weak."

If they had ever supposed that Jesus was somehow a spiritual superman, invincible to the weaknesses of the flesh, they beheld that night a very vulnerable human being.

As Mark would later write, "…he began to be deeply distressed and troubled. 'My soul is overwhelmed with sorrow to the point of death' he said to them." And though in the privacy of his prayer grove, they nonetheless could overhear him pray "Abba Father, everything is possible for you. Take this cup from me. Yet not what I will, but what you will."

In human terms his prayer was certainly understandable. We have all had occasion to ask God for something and in the same breath say that we surrender to his will, even if the outcome is not as we would wish it. But ever in the background is the tendency to exert self-will.

This time it was different! His life was on the line! He had testified "My will is to do the will of him that sent me." But was it even sane to hold to such a resolve under these circumstances?

It is little wonder that he returned to prayer a second time. It is perhaps to be expected that he prayed the same prayer yet again, and in his vulnerability once again returned to his three disciples for their prayer support, alas with the same results.

When Jesus returned, yet a third time, he realized that the souls of all mankind hung in the balance. "For this reason have I come."

Yes, Father Abraham lifted the knife of obedience to plunge into his son Isaac, believing that if God would do so he could raise Isaac to life again. But this time the knife would not be stopped!

Fail now and all hope of redemption would be lost. What a price to pay for the foolishness of wayward mankind!

And there it was! Not just another tussle with conscience, rather a spiritual battle-to-the-death with Satan the author of all that is evil.

In reflection, I am sure Satan's original words came back to him. "Turn these stones into bread." "Bow down and worship me." "Cast yourself off the pinnacle of the Temple." "Didn't I tell you that all the kingdoms of the earth are mine?" But this time the satanic attack was absolutely vicious.

"Here you are face to face with your so-called 'Father's will' and where is he? It's game over."

"All your good works and sanctimonious teaching are down the drain. The very people who profess to believe in you will in a few hours be crying 'Crucify him.' And what's more, if all the sins of the people are to be placed on you, and sin cannot enter Heaven, then I've got you! It's game over! I win!"

"And then there is the question of your suffering!"

"Have you any idea of the torment and agony of a death on a cross, not to mention the horrendous flogging with metal shards and jagged bone fastened to several lengths of leather strips, administered by calloused cruel Roman soldiers? And do you think it will be just forty stripes save one if ever you survive that many?"

"You'll carry the cross beam, or possibly the whole cross on the raw flesh of your shoulders, through the streets of Jerusalem to Golgotha, amid the jeering spiteful crowd, where they will nail you by the wrists to the cross beam, and drive a spike through both your feet entwined together, using seven inch spikes."

"You'll begin a slow painful death by asphyxia as the lungs fill with fluid, and to exhale is next to impossible. Your heart will increase its pumping to an excruciating speed possibly bursting from the pressure. Your twisted body will scream in agony no matter if it lift or sag to allow a breath."

"You'll hang there all but naked while the soldiers cast lots for your clothes. Above your head will be posted the sign that announces your crime. Your body will be left to rot on the cross, except in your case, it being your religious Passover, they may take your body down so as not to desecrate your so-called Sabbath. But to make sure you're dead they will break your legs to assure the asphyxiation and then for good measure they may even push a spear into your torso."

"Give it up Jesus! You're a goner! And the last remaining few of your so-called disciples will just slink away and leave your life's purpose in shambles."

It is little wonder that the always-inquisitive Peter, hearing the earnest agonizing of his Lord, parted the branches to Jesus' prayer grove so they beheld him exuding great blood-filled drops of sweat!

John confessed he had never heard, nor witnessed, such a prayer battle in all his life.

Then with great emotion he described the revelation of the divine nature of Gethsemane as before their very eyes an angel from heaven appeared to Jesus and strengthened him, and they all heard Jesus say, "Nevertheless not my will Father, but yours be done."

Then and only then did Jesus finally rise from Gethsemane's rock, determined to endure his cross!

Now his face was aglow with a divine presence as he came the third time to the three disciples, only this time to face the arresting officers.

"But," said John, "none of us were prepared for the hypocritical malevolence of the traitorous disciple as he approached Jesus."

"Judas, are you betraying the Son of Man with a kiss?"

Did the traitor hope to bring justification to his actions by an expression of regret that Jesus had to die for some supposed insurrection worthy of death?

Then Jesus asked them, "Who is it you want?" "Jesus of Nazareth," they replied. I am he," Jesus said.

The whole arresting party suddenly drew back, aghast, tripping over themselves and falling on the ground, as though they had seen some supernatural apparition.

This very thing happened a second time as they again mentioned his name.

As they got up on their feet yet again, bereft of any composure whatever, Jesus asked the question a third time, now permitting them to arrest him.

To protect Jesus, Peter drew that sword I had earlier seen under his cloak, and cut off the ear of the servant of the High Priest.

Jesus was instant to command that he put away the sword, and reached out and touched the wound of the servant, restoring his ear to its original state.

What the three disciples had discovered at Gethsemane was yet again confirmed at Jesus' arrest. There was no man that durst come against him, except by the divine permission of God and Jesus' own acquiescence to the suffering that lay ahead of him!

Jesus added further chagrin to the arrest!

He asked, "Am I leading a rebellion, that you have come with swords and clubs? Everyday I was with you in the temple courts, and you did not lay a hand on me." His inference of course was that they dared not arrest him amid the people who would have instantly come to his defense. That would indeed have started a riot that would have brought down the full force of Rome, endangering many lives and making a certain end to any semblance of Jewish self-rule.

He added, "But this is your hour – when darkness reigns." It was to be understood that even with all the powers of Heaven at his disposal, Jesus' surrender to his captors was completely voluntary. It was in response to what he believed was the will of his Heavenly Father for the completing of the final solution for sin.

He threw out one last challenge to them all, his disciples, the traitor Judas, and his captors. "Do you think I cannot call on my Father, and he will at once put at my disposal more than twelve legions of angels? But how then would the Scriptures be fulfilled that say it must happen in this way?"

Then he so lovingly removed the blame from the disciples who would soon forsake him.

They had their man. He was now in their custody. They had no quarrel with his disciples. "If you are looking for me, then let these men go."

Though there would certainly be self-recrimination in the heart of each of them, their infidelity would never be brought against them in this life or the next.

And then he willingly allowed them to bind him and take him to the moment for which he had been born.

"...But if I spoke the truth, why did you strike me?"

(John 18:23;)

CHAPTER 22

The Prosecutors

ON THE PRIOR instructions of the Sanhedrin, the Roman Centurion took Jesus to Annas, the High Priest emeritus. This was more ceremonial than official, a protocol in recognizing his illustrious service to Israel. It was preliminary to the actual trial to be conducted by Caiaphas, the present High Priest.

Annas was to officially lay the charges that would be brought against Jesus arising from his teachings and the activity of his disciples.

Jesus challenged Annas that he had openly taught the people by the thousands in the synagogues, in the Temple and on the Judean hillsides and beaches. Word of his teachings was by now reaching every corner of the known world, so why this secret arrest?

His was no secret society. Annas could ask anyone he cared to question about his teaching and his supporting miracles, right here and now! Then he could bring forward charges supported by legitimate witnesses.

One of the court officials struck Jesus in the face, accusing him of insubordination before the High Priest.

But the perpetrator was put on the spot!

"If I said something wrong, testify as to what is wrong," Jesus retorted. When the official could make no reply of accusation, Jesus asked, "But if I spoke the truth, why did you strike me?"

It was quite clear to Annas that he was no match for Jesus. He was only too happy to send him, still bound, to Caiaphas.

All of us members of the Sanhedrin, and a number of lawyers skilled in the interpretation of Jewish law, were assembled with Caiaphas awaiting the arrival of Jesus and his captors.

A number of potential witnesses were clustered together waiting their opportunity to speak against Jesus.

Because of the sanctity of our meeting place, and on account of the large rabble crowd that had been summoned, the trial was held in the grounds of the residence of the Chief Priest.

As an aside, let me explain that sanctity and head-counts weren't the only reasons for this outdoor exhibition.

You can read in your own Bible how feasts were held outdoors The more attention to be drawn to the lavishness of the host, the better. Passers-by, neighbors, and even the poor would witness the festivities and supposedly would think more highly of the man who could afford such extravagance. Does not this common trait continue in every society, as though any of us could take credit for the good fortune afforded us, as though by means of our own prowess we were specially favored?

Was there to be no recognition and thanksgiving to God for his part in bringing us to such a blessed estate?

But I continue!

Just as the arresting party arrived, the break of day appeared in the eastern sky, bringing the coolest temperatures of the night. A large bonfire was lit to gain some relief from the cold of the dawn.

My attention to the proceedings was momentarily distracted by a large bulk of a man, in clothes common to the Galilee region, who had come into the light of the fire, undoubtedly to warm himself. I was dumfounded to recognize him as the disciple Peter.

Evidently his obsessive curiosity had overcome his fear, and feeling safe within the crowd he had come to see the outcome of the trial.

I was not to know that this very night Peter would endure his own personal trial, accused by his own conscience, as the prophecy of Jesus concerning his denial of any knowledge of his Lord would be fulfilled.

I leave the details of his spiritual suffering to other writers, save to say that he had evidently denied his association with Jesus no less than three times that night, and I personally saw Jesus turn and look at Peter just as a rooster crowed the dawn of a new day.

True to the loving character of Jesus, Peter later acknowledged the bitter tears he had wept, and the forgiveness and reinstatement to ministry his master had given him.

But I must get on with my story.

I have earlier referred to the dictatorial nature of the proceedings of the Sanhedrin. But on this night the rancor and unadulterated savagery of raw power that this assembly was to perpetrate in the name of religion would bring the greatest disgrace upon our nation that we had ever known. The task was clear! We were to condemn the "Son of God" to death, despite the lack of legitimate evidence.

Whether rehearsed or spontaneous, it does not matter, the many witnesses who spoke against him proved to be in contradiction one to the other, and certainly no accusation worthy of his execution had been brought forward.

Despite their anticipation, those members of the Sanhedrin who were against Jesus could not find any accusation that could rise above the level of absolute absurdity.

Then, as though awaiting their much anticipated début in the wings, two witnesses were brought to center stage to say that they had heard Jesus say, "I am able to destroy the temple of God and rebuild it in three days."

Couched in the terms these witnesses had put it, the intent of Jesus certainly seemed to be a threat to do just that.

We had no idea then that he was speaking of his eventual resurrection from the dead.

We all recalled Jesus' words he had uttered in the temple after he had physically rid it of the commercial stalls and moneychangers, calling it a "den of thieves."

It was not Jesus who threatened to destroy the temple. He had told us clearly "(*If you*) destroy this temple…"

He would be its savior, not its destroyer!

No! Jesus had a far greater proof of his divinity in mind, than to merely rebuild stone and mortar by miraculous means.

From other-minded witnesses we knew that he had literally walked on water; instantly calmed the stormy sea; withered a fig tree with a single command; fed over eight thousand people from a young lad's lunch of just a few loaves and two fish, and the meager rations of his disciples.

Not to mention the hundreds, perhaps thousands across our country that could be brought forward to demonstrate their healing that Jesus had performed upon them.

And what could we say if he had produced those he had raised from the dead?

You can be certain these potential witnesses knew nothing of these proceedings.

Notwithstanding, the greatest evidence of his divine authority was yet to come. And we would be party to its disclosure.

As John later wrote in his gospel, "But the Temple he had spoken of was his body."

Little wonder then that Jesus made no reply. Untruths are never exposed by self-defense.

As you can see, the greatest care had been taken to avoid any inference concerning Jesus' claim to divinity.

To ask Jesus if he was the Christ, the Messiah, would further expose their unbelief, or worse, their outright rejection of the one for whom their nation had waited for over four hundred years. But it was the only basis upon which they could justify the death sentence. Blasphemy!

For my part, despite the sadness that plagued my heart, I could not see the delay in asking the question. We all knew that Caiaphas would have his way despite the overwhelming evidence to Jesus' claim.

Jesus needed only to maintain his silence until the question was raised; the charge that would bring condemnation, not to Jesus, but upon our whole nation. The damning outburst of the acting High Priest, soon to come, would become the scourge of our nation, as thirty years hence Jewish blood would flow across our land, and our people would once again be driven from Israel into countries around the world in a disbursement that would last almost two thousand years, fulfilling the warnings of our own prophets.

Caiaphas would not relent. "If you are the Christ, tell us." Not a question, but a dare!

But Jesus was ready for him. "If I tell you, you will not believe me, and if I asked you, you would not answer."

Finally there was nothing for it! We all heard it! Caiaphas commanded Jesus straight out, "I charge you under oath by the living God: tell us if you are the Christ, the Son of God."

He had uttered the feared words at last.

Now Jesus could answer the High Priest, with all the authority of the Kingdom of God. "Yes, it is as *you* say," Jesus replied. "But I say to all of you: In the future you will see the Son of Man sitting at the right hand of the Mighty One and coming on the clouds of heaven."

Note the important difference in the two statements! By his inference the High Priest had acknowledged Jesus to be the Son of God, a position of divine relationship that made Jesus equal with God. Throughout his ministry Jesus had never referred to his earthly existence in any other terms but that he was the "Son of man."

To condemn him, Caiaphas by his own admission would deny the very Messiah for whom we all waited.

It was then that literally "all Hell broke loose!"

"...Yes, it is as you say,..."

(Luke 23:3;)

CHAPTER 23

Supreme Court

I⊤ was hay-day in Hell! First the traitor; Now the accuser; Next the Christ! A one-two-three knockout if ever there was one.

"I told you so!" So, in retrospect, I fancy the taunting of Satan upon Jesus as he crossed the point of no return.

One would have thought a simple "yes" would do! If Jesus had only remained silent after that, then the denial that he was the Son of God would have brought the sole guilt upon Caiaphas. The burden of proof was his to prove that Jesus was not who he said he was.

Now, Jesus had brought solid evidence of his divine relationship to God through his miracles performed. But still he was not believed. He had prophesied his resurrection from the grave in three days time. But that was a wait-and-see situation. Now he would proclaim the consequences of that divine miracle.

"But I say to all of you: In the future you will see the Son of Man sitting at the right hand of the Mighty One and coming on the clouds of heaven." That is an event that has been waited for by many subsequent generations, including yours.

It was at this point that the participants in this trial traded positions. It was the Sanhedrin that was now on trial, not Jesus.

If I took a position that Jesus was the Christ, it would have to be an act of faith! And if I ruled against him he would have my answer.

For the first time in my political life I was glad that a ballot was not going to be required of me, because the acting High Priest had resolved the problem for me.

It was then that he tore his clothes (a Jewish custom that demonstrated profound offense) and said, "He has spoken blasphemy! Why do we need any more witnesses? Look, now you have heard the blasphemy. What do you think?"

As if to deflect any guilt from self, he allowed the judicial body to proclaim the only verdict available to them. "He is worthy of death."

The verdict did not come from a headcount this time. The uproar of the Sanhedrin, joined by the cries of the rabble crowd implied a unanimous agreement that Jesus should be put to death.

Let me assure you that there were some voices in the Sanhedrin that remained mute when the question was raised.

Do I mean to imply by this that we were innocent of the murderous plot? No! Mark my word! Silence is never a vote in any direction. If we believed Jesus was the Christ, then at some point we were going to have to declare ourselves and risk the consequences.

It was at this point where things really got out of hand. Whether egged on by any of the judicial body I do not know, but the rabble crowd lunged forward and attacked Jesus, spitting in his face, slapping and even punching him in the face with their fists, daring him to "Prophecy to us, Christ, Who hit you?"

I cannot imagine the guilt and remorse that will confront them when before the judgment seat of heaven they will be called by name and will confess what they did.

It was fortunate for Jesus that the Roman Centurion stepped in and ordered him to be held under their protection. But as we shall see, that protection was short lived.

Now, the authorization of the death penalty by crucifixion lay exclusively with the Roman Governor, Pilate! And despite the early hour, the Chief Priest, and the Sanhedrin, followed by the rabble crowd, paraded Jesus off to the governor's palace.

It might seem strange that Pilate would tolerate such a rude awakening, and that he would conduct his trial of Jesus in the outer courtyard instead of in his throne room.

Let me explain!

This particular morning was the beginning of the day of preparation for the greatest religious celebration of the Jewish calendar that would commence at sundown. Passover!

It commemorated the crossing of the Red Sea by the Hebrew slaves that had served the Egyptian Pharaohs for four hundred and thirty years.

The Jews were to prepare their home and their person through ritual cleansing for the eating of the Passover meal that very night. They were not to defile themselves by contact with any non-Jewish person, things, or property, until after the conclusion of the celebration.

Pilate must acquiesce to the demands of this Jewish High Holiday despite the inconvenience.

Today, in particular, he would placate the people by means of special attention to their religious hierarchy. He would even release a Jewish prisoner of their choice, should he have one in custody at the time.

This interruption at such an outrageous hour primed him with anticipation of some serious matter that could not wait the normal protocol. Indeed, the presence and clamor of such a large crowd was in itself unnerving.

It is safe to say that the din most certainly must have awakened the whole household of the palace, as we shall soon see, most fortuitous!

The Chief Priests were certainly aware that the presentation of their case must represent some threat to the security and serenity of the nation and a threat to Roman rule. Pilate could care less for the religious nuances of our race, except that they somehow rendered our nation to be the most difficult area to rule in all the occupied territory of the Roman world.

In fact, no doubt thinking their complaint would be of a religious nature, and wanting to get on with matters more important to Rome, he dismissed the lawyers, telling them to judge the case for themselves.

The lawyers assured Pilate that their case was of a criminal nature requiring the death sentence.

Now this was the crux of the matter. The Romans tolerated executions by the Jews of persons found guilty of crimes against Jewish law, a case in point being the stoning to death of women caught in prostitution and adultery.

Jesus had defended such a woman by sheer appeal to the conscience of the men who condemned her.

Normally, the Jews would have stoned Jesus to death on the pretext of blasphemy, or any other charge they might find convenient. But only Rome held the power of execution by crucifixion, and that was what the Jewish leaders were after.

So, as predictably as they were false, our lawyers laid charges against Jesus before Pilate that would force him to take jurisdiction.

"We have found this man subverting our nation. He opposes payment of taxes to Caesar and claims to be Christ a King."

Note the contradictions!

The High Priest had accused Jesus of blasphemy against God, a purely religious accusation that demanded death by stoning. There was nothing politically seditious or subverting about that.

As for not paying taxes, this was a blatant lie. They could well recall the outcome of the last time they would ever challenge Jesus, as I have earlier mentioned in detail.

The final accusation was as blasphemous as it was false. Remember Caiaphas had asked Jesus "Are you then the Son of God?" The question had nothing to do with Rome.

Now they were taking their Messiah, their Christ, and reducing him to that of a puppet king, like Herod, when their historic national expectations were that the Messiah would liberate their nation from their Roman conquerors.

Of course Pilate picked up on that one. "Are you the king of the Jews?"

Jesus replied, "Yes, it is as you say."

The Jewish leaders were now wringing their hands with glee. Now they had him. Pilate could not possibly deny the threat to the Roman Empire.

But they had not counted on the secret intervention of Pilate's wife who they boasted publicly was favorable toward their religion.

Having heard the accusations from the Chief Priest, as presented by our lawyers, and since there was no one to publicly stand in Jesus' defense, Pilate retreated into the privacy of the palace to further question Jesus.

"....My kingdom is not of this world..."

(John 18:36;)

CHAPTER 24

In Defense

S ANITY OR INSANITY, I plead to neither! But as soon as I heard Jesus' answer to this last accusation, some overwhelming influence, be it mind or spirit I do not know, gripped me and I found myself, at great risk, slinking away from the crowd, propelled toward a remote entrance to the palace.

Thinking I was on official business, the guard readily admitted me and I made my way discreetly to the room where Pilate's court officials were gathered.

I knew then why I had come!

Without prior intention, God helping me, I was going to give evidence in favor of Jesus!

Pilate had listened to the sham of accusations the Chief Priest had presented. Was there no one who could or would stand in defense of Jesus?

It was at this point that I asked for permission to speak.

I explained that as a member of the Sanhedrin (a fact familiar to Pilate) I was bound to tell him that the Sanhedrin was not unanimous in the presentation of our accusations against Jesus. There were in fact a few of us, self included, that believed that there was no justification for the accusations he had heard this morning. Jesus' claim to kingship was spiritual in nature and held no threat either to Judea or to Rome.

The accusation of breaking the Jewish Sabbath was raised as a mere technicality in the hopes of persuading the Governor of some threat to Rome.

I then reminded him that the rabble crowd outside had been previously concocted, or otherwise would never even be aware of these proceedings at this early hour because they would be at home tending to the business of preparing for the Passover just hours away.

This also explained why there were no witnesses present to come to Jesus' defense.

I felt it my place to bring to Pilate's attention a few highlights of Jesus' benevolent ministry among the sick.

I told him of the day a man, crippled from birth, was lowered by his friends down through the roof of the house where Jesus was engaged in his teaching and healing ministry. Unperturbed, Jesus had healed the man, who then walked for the first time in his life.

I told Pilate about the blind man who only a few days ago had received his sight as he sat by the roadside as Jesus passed by; his healing of the woman who had suffered with an issue of blood for many years; the numbers of demon-possessed people that Jesus had successfully exorcised.

Then I gave a detailed account of his raising Lazarus from the dead.

I assured Pilate that Jesus had never once in our hearing ever spoken against Rome.

I finally explained to Pilate how Jesus had incurred the wrath of the High Priest and a large number of us Pharisees by defending the rights of the common people to worship God in our temple without prohibitive social, economic and religious requirements (as earlier explained).

I could hardly believe my ears! What was I saying?

These were words that would easily stand as blasphemous to the High Priest as did the words of Jesus, for I was one of *them*!

Or was I?

You might by now think that I had become a "believer" having taken this course of action. But were I to even hint at such conviction, as do all true believers, I would discover that the proof of faith in Christ lies in counting the cost and paying the price of allegiance by my divesting of every trace of self-interest.

In all honesty I must confess that I had not reached that point as yet!

It was then that Pilate's wife came to the room and passed a note to a high official and asked him to deliver it immediately to Pilate.

In fact she was aware of the miracle performing ministry of Jesus that dominated the conversation of her circle of high society women, a number of who were wives of the Jewish hierarchy.

I learned later she had not had a good night's sleep. She had tossed and turned all night suffering from a dream that warned of the dire circumstances that would come to her husband and to all of Rome, should he convict Jesus and sentence him to death by crucifixion. All this before the Sanhedrin had even brought Jesus to Pilate.

Her note stated that she had been warned in her dream that Jesus was innocent, and that her husband must not have anything to do with this obvious charade of a trial.

It was her note that alerted Pilate of the need to acquit Jesus of any crime against his jurisdiction. He must, at all cost, set him free.

He once again asked Jesus, "Are you the king of the Jews?"

At that point Jesus turned the very question back on Pilate. "Is that your own idea," Jesus asked, "or did others talk to you about me?"

I could not help but gain the impression that Jesus was seeking out the very soul of Pilate. Did Pilate seek solely the placating of Jewish justice, or could it be possible that he desired to know the answer for his own soul's sake?

Now here was a conundrum! There was a Jewish King already on the throne, a puppet king to be sure, but a king nonetheless.

His name was Herod. He retained some restricted authority in the district of Galilee, although claiming jurisdiction throughout all of Judea, a presumption that put him at cross-purposes with Rome, and in particular, Pilate, who was governor of the entire country. There was no love lost between these two potentates.

He was the son of the original King Herod who had ordered the slaughter of the male babies of Bethlehem and region, up to two years of age, in an attempt to wipe out the threat of any Messianic King that would depose or succeed him.

In retrospect, I seem to think that this conflict between the two men gave Jesus some leverage. If his claim was entitlement to the Judean throne, and were it to be upheld by Pilate, who had authority to appoint who he wished, then he would have to release Jesus as the true heir to the Jewish throne.

Now wouldn't that scenario be a tempting way to goad Herod into creating a protest that would in turn give Pilate grounds for deposing him?

With this question, Jesus reminded Pilate of the immense responsibility that was his in determining his guilt or innocence. In reality Pilate was as much on trial as was Jesus, indeed as were all of us involved in this nightmare!

"Am I a Jew?" Pilate retorted. "It was your own people and your chief priests who handed you over to me. What is it you have done?"

It was then that Jesus gave vent to what this trial was all about.

"My kingdom is not of this world. If it were my servants would fight to prevent my arrest by the Jews. But now my kingdom is from another place."

Once again Pilate was reminded of the tenuousness of this moment. Undoubtedly he had heard considerable from his wife, and perhaps a few of his household, a number of whom it seems were sympathetic to Jesus, about the thousands throughout his jurisdiction who, if they knew what proceedings eluded them would undoubtedly come to the aid of Jesus.

If Pilate feared a riot from the rabble crowd outside, he could certainly surmise a national uprising of persons far and wide who held to the fact that Jesus was the Messiah.

But Jesus had never submitted to the fickle whims of the majority, who he realized could and would change sides and cower to the religious leaders for no other reason than they seemed to be winning.

Then too, could Pilate have been told by the Roman Centurion in charge of Jesus' arrest, how Jesus claimed that he could command twelve legions of heavenly angels to come to his rescue?

Had he heard from the same source how Jesus had rebuked the disciple that drew his sword at his arrest, and even restored the ear of the High Priest's servant?

Did Pilate know that Jesus had prevented his disciples from resisting arrest and persuaded the Centurion that they should be set free?

It seemed to me that "the other place" Jesus referred to must have shaken Pilate to his very bootstraps, because there were clearly no grounds to convict him of treason against the Roman Empire.

But to Pilate the issue was not yet satisfied.

"You are a king, then!" said Pilate. "A king of what?" That was the question.

Jesus then asserted his claim to royalty. "You are right in saying I am a king. In fact for this reason I was born, and for this reason I came into the world, to testify to the truth. Everyone on the side of truth listens to me."

"What is truth?" retorted Pilate! "Wrong Question Pilate!"

With that, Pilate left Jesus inside and returned to his accusers. "Poor timing Pilate!" There could have been no greater opportunity afforded him to come into the truth.

If only Pilate had asked "*Who* is truth?" If only he had not yielded to his own cynicism aggravated by the years of petty pretenders to power, such as awaited him out in the courtyard.

Or had his own ambitions been thwarted so completely as to send him into this most inconspicuous region on the edge of the Empire? Was his status with Rome so precarious that the judgment now before him teetered between truth and expediency?

"What is truth Pilate?"

I learned some time later that a humble disciple of Jesus, named Thomas, full of doubts and confusion over the impending crisis Jesus had just announced, asked the right question. "Lord we don't know where you are going, so how can we know the way?"

He received the answer that Pilate so desperately needed and would have received if he had paused for just a moment's delay.

Jesus had answered Thomas, "I am the way and the truth and the life. No one comes to the Father except through me. If you really knew me, you would know my Father as well. From now on, you do know him and have seen him."

"I find no basis for a charge against this man," said Pilate.

He had made the right assessment of his prisoner, but he had no idea why that was!

With that, the Chief Priest broadened the charges to include inciting the Jews throughout Judea. "He started in Galilee and has come all the way here."

It was too good to be true! Jesus' accusers had just given him a way out!

Pilate would send Jesus to Herod, who conveniently happened to be in Jerusalem at the time, undoubtedly to celebrate the Passover.

Let Herod do the dirty work! It was guaranteed that he would not tolerate any pretender to his throne! He would convict Jesus faster than he could snap his fingers, and Pilate could then, in the privacy of his palace, sign the authorization for his execution by crucifixion.

Should, inconceivably, Herod not convict Jesus, his assessment and recommendation for pardon would reinforce Pilate's decision to free Jesus with a stern warning against inciting public unrest, with a good whipping to ensure his compliance.

The involvement of Herod in the trial most surely would placate the Sanhedrin, would it not?

Now I do not want to depict Herod as being as intellectually bereft as were his scruples. Jesus himself had referred to him on one occasion as "that old fox." But it was his dark soul syndrome that seemed to lack any spiritual interest whatever in the possibility that Jesus might just be the long awaited Messiah, that I believe caused him to treat Jesus as a curiosity.

In any case, Pilate made out that the offense, supposedly having originated in Galilee, should be tried by Herod's court. And so off went the High Priest and the Sanhedrin, followed by the rabble crowd, to Herod's Jerusalem residence.

Well, if flattery will get you anywhere!

Herod was ecstatic at such an auspicious opportunity to finally meet Jesus for the first time. He had long desired to see him, and if the rumors were true, it might be possible that Jesus would perform one of his miracles just for him.

He questioned Jesus in great detail, but to his chagrin, Jesus made no response, not a word!

But there was no letup from the Chief Priest and most of the Sanhedrin. They had brought along Jesus' accusers and false witnesses to see if Herod might buy into their scheme, even if Pilate had not done so.

Not all of us joined in believe me. We who protested this sham rolled our eyes in dismay at the incredulity of those who pretended to be the guardians of our faith.

It obviously never occurred to Herod that Jesus was any sort of threat to his throne, much less that he was the actual "babe" his infamous ancestor had tried to murder. Indeed Jesus' claim to be a king was most humorous, given that his hometown was Nazareth. Everybody in Galilee and beyond chided, "can any good thing come out of Nazareth?"

Herod, assuming that Jesus' lack of response must mean him to be a charlatan, began to mock him, and because of his claim to be a king, put an elegant purple robe on his shoulders and sent him back to Pilate.

Though not as yet apparent, there was soon to be added to his attire a crown!

"...You would have no power over me..."

(John 19:11;)

CHAPTER 25

A Trade-Off

THE INTERRUPTION OF his breakfast had given considerable annoyance to Pilate. After such an unprecedented start to his day he was most happy to be rid of Jesus and the rabble crowd, to say nothing of those insufferable priests.

Surely Herod would take care of the matter and his involvement in this case would pave the way to improved relations with the royal court. In fact, as it turned out, those relationships almost instantly burst into a considerable friendship between the two.

Meanwhile just the thought of the High Priest having to bow to that rogue of a king was enough to place a curt smile on Pilate's face.

But here he was again, this Jesus of Nazareth; And certainly at the most inconvenient moment after his first appearance.

Well, "time for plan B," thought Pilate.

Herod had neither arrested nor sentenced Jesus under Jewish law. It could only mean that he also had found no grounds for the accusations placed before him. Jesus was as good as a free man!

But Pilate was about to be exposed as the epitome of convenience over justice.

Oh it was not that he did not make a noticeable attempt to release Jesus, a sign that he at least recognized his obligation to uphold the law. He would face those phony accusers at least three times in an effort to release Jesus - as if he needed their consent in any case!

Once more he stood before the Jews, now prepared to give his final judgment in the matter.

He addressed the crowd.

"You brought me this man as one who was inciting the people to rebellion. I have examined him in your presence and have found no basis for your charges against him. Neither has Herod, for he sent him back to me; as you can see, he has done nothing to deserve death. Therefore, I will punish him and then release him."

What an unprecedented uproar reached Pilate's ears as, spurred on by the High Priest, the rabble crowd shouted "Crucify him. Crucify him."

But Pilate was not yet exhausted of options.

As per the custom previously mentioned, he had not as yet released a Jewish prisoner, selected by the High Priest at the annual Feast of Pentecost.

From the Jewish perspective, this act was a benevolent expression of the forgiveness of sin, apropos to the most holy day on the Jewish calendar.

From the Roman point of view this was an act of compassion, made by the Roman Governor in lip service to the religion of this enemy-occupied country.

Now as before mentioned, this year Pilate had in custody probably the most notorious prisoner ever captured. Truly he was a prize to be had and most useful to Pilate in achieving the accolades of Caesar.

I was awed with the irony that Pilate should bate the accusers with a choice between Barabbas, a murderer, and Jesus, who was obviously innocent. Surely he must rule "no match" between an insurrectionist and a king, and let Jesus go.

Would history record the most infamous act of treachery ever committed upon God and man; that the highest religious seat of authority in all Jewry would extinguish the greatest life ever lived, in favor of their own power, and forever earn the disgust of all so-called "pagan nations?"

Surely we would not go so far as that! Could there be any greater proof of our arrogance and hypocrisy?

With finality, Pilate addressed the crowd.

"I find no basis for a charge against him, but it is your custom for me to release to you one prisoner at the time of the Passover. Do you want me to release 'the king of the Jews'?"

But to his amazement, the rabble crowd, prompted by the High Priest, shouted back, "No, not him! Give us Barabbas!"

Pilate was cornered! His strategy had backfired! There was no possible way out of this conundrum. The all-consuming priority now, was to save face, with the Jews, and with Rome!

To release Jesus was to precipitate a full-blown riot! To release Barabbas was to face the possible displeasure of Rome.

Which decision would hold the most justification?

How shrewd the mind becomes when cornered!

Let Barabbas go – for now – in time he would be at it again and Rome would waste no time in making a swift execution and terrorize the populace into submission.

Double accolades! A riot averted and a terrorist executed! What matter that Pilate's guilt would mingle with Jewish blood?

Despite having given his official ruling of innocence, Pilate was left with no other recourse but to have Jesus flogged per the usual procedure common to Roman justice.

The problem was that Pilate had no personal oversight of that procedure. Besides, it was the minimum sentence pronounced on prisoners, whether pronounced innocent or guilty.

The following details I received later from the Roman Centurion.

There stood Jesus, regaled in his purple robe, before the soldiers appointed to the grisly task. They were swift to take advantage of his "regal" apparel and in no time plated a crown of thorns, made from a Euphorbiacene bush, and, with full knowledge of its potential pain, forced it down on Jesus' head.

It was a bush common to the area, used as a hedge, its thick barbarous thorns effectively keeping at bay any stray animals.

It was a bloody scene indeed! But nothing compared to the unprecedented agony he was about to endure.

Now may I add, this "Roman" flogging, I have already described earlier, bore no comparison to a "Jewish" flogging, a common punishment for offences against the breaking of some religious rules. For one thing, we administered only thirty-nine lashes of forty in the care that the law not be broken.

The Roman lashing was merciless and all too often the prisoner died from the shock resulting from the pain and damage to the body.

The Centurion further explained that, having survived the lashing, Jesus was once again arrayed in his "royal" robe; a staff was put in his hand; and the soldiers knelt in mock obeisance saying "Hail king of the Jews!" striking him repeatedly in the face.

When Jesus was returned to Pilate, those of us assembled with him in the palace were aghast at his suffering.

I then surreptitiously made my way back to the courtyard to join my colleagues, admitting to myself the horror of what awaited Jesus.

As I took my place, without explanation for my absence, I saw Pilate appear alone before the crowd to address them.

"Look, I am bringing him out to you to let you know that I find no basis for a charge against him," he said.

Pilate then had Jesus brought out to stand before the crowd, held erect by a soldier on each side of him; blood, from his head, oozing over his regal robe, the staff still clutched in his hand.

"Here is the man!" shouted Pilate as though to draw attention to his intention to release Jesus, now that he had been flogged.

He was met with one word that began with the Chief Priest, the members of the Sanhedrin joining in, and soon amplified

by seemingly every voice in the crowd. "Crucify!" "Crucify!"
But let me assure you there were a few mute voices amongst the
Sanhedrin, mine among them!

Fully aware of his sarcasm, Pilate retorted, "You take him and
crucify him. As for me, I find no basis for a charge against him."
As if they had any power to act without Pilate's consent!

The Jewish lawyers retorted. "We have a law, and according
to that law he must die, because he claimed to be the Son of
God."

Now the tables were turned from Pilate's jurisdiction to what
the Jews held to be a superior jurisdiction, "Rabbinical Law."

If Pilate was unnerved by the potential for the riot of this
crowd, he was now even more afraid for a full-blown national
uprising that his obvious flagrant contempt for Jewish authority
might incite.

But an even larger issue consumed Pilate!

Notwithstanding his disregard for the Jewish religion, he was
superstitious enough to envision that amid the myriad of Roman
gods, Jesus could possibly be some legitimate god he had never
heard of.

Pilate hastily removed himself and Jesus to the safety of the
palace once again and asked Jesus outright, "Where do you come
from?"

Jesus gave him no answer, in Pilate's view, an act of contempt
of the court.

"Do you refuse to speak to me? Don't you realize I have power
either to free or to crucify you?"

Jesus then, in characteristic fashion, absolved Pilate of any
offence against him.

"You would have no power over me if it were not given to
you from above. Therefore the one who handed me over to you
is guilty of the greater sin."

There were two issues of resolve here.

First, Jesus reminded Pilate that his authority issued from
Rome. It was alone facilitated by Caesar. Pilate would only be

carrying out the expected duty of his office. There was no offense here.

But the second issue was a matter for Pilate's conscience.

Jesus, if he were a person of divine authority, had at his disposal the right and the disposition of divine intervention to thwart his execution; an event that would not only save his life, but would simultaneously dissolve all human authority, be it Roman, Jewish or any other.

It was up to Pilate to determine for himself which course of action to take.

Pilate must have marveled that Jesus had exercised no such prerogative. But for whatever his reasoning, to his credit he used every legal recourse available to him to set Jesus free.

His obligation to Caesar now became a weapon of choice for the astute legal representatives of the Sanhedrin. They declared, "If you let this man go, you are no friend of Caesar. Anyone who claims to be a king opposes Caesar."

It mattered not what empire Jesus might claim to represent, be it divine or human. Pilate's allegiance to Caesar was imperative!

Jesus himself had made clear passage for Pilate. He had said in effect, "Do what you have to do!"

And so he did!

Pilate then had Jesus brought outside before the seat of judgment and once again declared that Jesus was in his view innocent.

The crescendo of anger rose to an all-time volume. "Crucify him! Crucify him!"

The Jewish lawyers now made their final argument.

Not only had they reminded Caesar of his official obligation to the Roman Emperor, they now denigrated their own nation to the sovereignty of their enemy. "This man has claimed to be a king. *But we have no king but Caesar.* If you release this Jesus, you are no friend of Caesar!"

Still, Pilate made his final appeal.

Asking for the traditional bowl of water, he sat in the seat of judgment, and washing his hands declared, "I am innocent of this man's blood. It is your responsibility."

To his utter amazement, spurred on by the Chief Priest he heard the whole assembly of Jews cry out *"Let his blood be on us and on our children."*

With one damnable sentence, the High Priest had sentenced, not Jesus, but the whole Jewish nation into utter banishment for almost two thousand years.

A people, no longer in agony for the bondage of their country, were soon to become a race *without* a country, her citizens dispersed amid the myriad of nations that encircle our globe.

Without a shepherd! Without hope! They would join the ranks of the nations they had so spurned as pagan, awaiting the day of the coming of the King of Kings and Lord of Lords to rule the earth. And he would be none other than Jesus of Nazareth, the very man they now condemned to death!

"...Daughters of Jerusalem, do not weep for me;..."

(Luke 23:28;)

CHAPTER 26

Let The Parade Begin

WITHOUT POMP OR circumstance, as though it was just another day in the courts, Jesus was led off by his Roman guards to take up his cross.

The place of the execution was on the hill of Golgotha, which means "the place of the skull." In reality it was an outcropping of the city dump that has the geological appearance of a human skull, aptly named, given the ignominious decay that would come from the executed corpses duly stripped of their flesh by vultures and various animals of prey.

The body or skeleton was removed for burial if requested by family or other concerned persons. Whenever necessary, it was removed by the authorities to make room for the next victims. The remains then became a part of the regular debris.

The exception was at Passover, when, in deference to the Jewish holy day, all bodies were removed before sunset, the beginning of the Day of Atonement. Such would be the case on this occasion.

Usually the upright beam of the cross was left anchored into the earth for convenience, the crossbeam carried to the site by the convicted criminal.

On this occasion there were two upright beams on the hill, one short of the three required, as two thieves were to be crucified with Jesus. This meant that one of the prisoners would have to bear the complete cross to his execution.

That Jesus was picked for this task serves only to show the calloused indifference of his executioners. Evil will always appear its strongest when the threat of redemption crosses its shadow.

A Satan-prompted travesty from start to finish, only the most ignominious treatment possible would satisfy him who in the very heavenly presence of the divine had blasphemed the God of all Creation. When such rears its head amid human kind it is literally "Hell on earth!"

Such abject abuse as had been administered to Jesus had left him physically unable to bear such a load as this. Why not use one of the other prisoners, presumably of stronger physique?

If the idea ever entered the mind of the Roman Centurion in charge of the execution, his indifference toward his beleaguered victim won the day.

Such inhumanity can only be equated with the vehemence of the enemy of the soul. Jesus would carry his cross to the place of his execution!

He was stripped of his "royal" robe and his regular clothes were put on him, and the most noble journey ever taken by man began; A journey of only 4/10th of a mile, or 650 meters, along Jerusalem streets that would become known as the Via Dolorosa – The Way of Grief, through the western gate, terminating at Golgotha where his presence would forever change the derision of its reputation from a place of refuse to a place of redemption – a place they called "Calvary" which means "the place of a scull;" but since has become perhaps the sweetest word in the Christian vocabulary, save for the precious name of Jesus, our Savior.

The sun was now fully risen and the city astir.

To be sure, both those sympathetic to Jesus, and those of the rabble crowd, had preceded the Roman detachment to all parts of the city to tell of the event taking place; Some excited by the thought of a triple execution; others to learn with unbelief that their beloved benefactor was among the accused.

The city streets, busy at any time of day, were by now crowded with last-minute shoppers in preparation for the Passover meal, now only some four hours away.

Those streets enfolded many heavy hearts reflected in tear-stained faces, and yes not a few reflecting outright anger that they had been denied the notice of what should have been a public trial in which witnesses for the defense most certainly would have to be called.

By this time it was too late! They could only watch in remorse as Jesus of Nazareth passed by. Now he could never be king!

If they could only have known that by sundown he would be their Savior!

As was the custom, the Chief Priests and members of the Sanhedrin, as Jesus' accusers, were required to follow the soldiers and their prisoners to the site of the execution.

This was no affront, because it afforded the Chief Priest and his entourage the opportunity to be seen by the crowds of people, who had come from near and far, for this most prestigious holy day of the year.

But amid that despicable display, I assure you, were some of our number who paraded in sympathy with the prisoner and those weeping souls on the sidelines.

It was totally predictable! Jesus had barely walked outside the palace grounds before he stumbled under the weight of his cross. But there would be no Roman muscle exercised on his behalf. Time to conscript the help of the first unsuspecting, "Atlas," that came along!

His name was Simon. He came from Cyrene, the provincial capital of Cyrenaica in the country of Libya in North Africa. It borders the Mediterranean Sea and is neighbor to Egypt.

John Mark was later to tell us that Simon had two sons, Alexander and Rufus, who, because of the dramatic change in the life of their father, after this experience, would become converts to Christ in the church that Simon himself would establish in Libya. It became apparent to me, following the crucifixion, that Simon's role in this dramatic episode of his life had wrought an enormous change in his persona. No other man was any closer to Jesus throughout this drama than was Simon of Cyrene!

Being the favorite disciple of Jesus, it was natural that the disciple John should, upon fleeing from arrest, go back to the Mount of Olives, to the general encampment of the disciple's entourage and report, first to Mary the mother of Jesus, and then to all of them, that Jesus had been convicted of false accusations and condemned to crucifixion.

John took personal charge of Mary, and the women in the group made their way to Jerusalem just in time to see the procession to Golgotha.

Careful to avoid any identity, John, with Mary and the women, watched as Jesus passed by.

John told me later he was certain that the gaze of Jesus penetrated the crowd and met squarely with the tearful eyes of his mother. But of course no sign of recognition, much less exchange of words could be made at that point.

For thirty-three years Mary, with haunting confusion, had held in her heart the words of the eminent old Simeon who had held her babe in his arms and declared Jesus to be the promised Messiah, the anointed one of God, a fulfillment of the divine promise of the Holy Spirit made to Simeon, that he would see the Messiah before his own demise.

"Sovereign Lord, as you have promised, you now dismiss your servant in peace. For my eyes have seen your salvation, which you have prepared in the sight of all people, a light for revelation to the Gentiles and for glory to your people Israel."

But Simeon, having blessed the parents, then said to Mary, "This child is destined to cause the falling and rising of many in Israel, and to be a sign that will be spoken against, so that the thoughts of many hearts will be revealed. A sword will pierce your own soul too."

They were words that seemed out of place on such an occasion as the dedication to God of their child at the Temple.

Even the venerable old Anna the prophetess, filled with excitement by the pronouncement of Simeon, skipped around the temple courtyard like a schoolgirl, telling good news she simply could not contain.

But what could such an ominous statement mean? "A sword piercing my own soul?" How often had Mary pondered his words about her son as she proudly watched him embrace the teachings of Moses from early youth?

She recalled often the bittersweet memory of finding their son amid the teachers of the law in the temple, two days missing from the entourage from Nazareth as they were heading home. As annoyed as she was with him, she could not help but be proud of the accolades these learnéd scholars shared with Joseph and her.

There had been times over the last three years when she was very concerned for the rivalry he seemed to have engendered between himself and the Pharisees in the course of his ministry.

The common people of course adored him, and the praise and thanksgiving afforded him by those he healed and exorcised was at times overwhelming, and of special chagrin to the scribes and Pharisees.

But a sword! Ah yes, a sword! Now she knew what Simeon had meant! Her heart bled for the agony of every step her son was taking under the weight of that cross, every step stabbing her own heart with the literal pain of sorrow.

Yes! Now she knew!

The blood trickled down Jesus' face from the impressions of his thorny crown, and the sweat engendered from the heat and toil of that day mingled with the blood soaking the shoulders of his garments.

If only she could help her son, but she could not!

Acting on a sudden impulse she reached into her apron pocket and produced a handkerchief and pressing forward to a woman standing in the front row of the crowd said, "Here! Give him this!"

The woman moved quickly because Jesus had almost past her. He could not grasp it, but it slid across his face wiping the grime from his eyes as he passed. She never returned the hanky, because Mary and John had moved on down farther following the procession to Golgotha.

As suddenly as it was unexpected, the words of Isaiah the prophet came to the woman; "He had no beauty or majesty to attract us to him, nothing in his appearance that we should desire him. He was despised and rejected by men, a man of sorrows, and familiar with suffering. Like one from whom men hide their faces he was despised, and we esteemed him not."

I was of course aware of the commotion up ahead of me because the soldiers had very quickly pushed the woman quite briskly back into the crowd. But I could not see what had happened. John later filled me in with the details I have just mentioned.

I could not know at the time that I would see this woman again!

It was not long past this scene that Jesus stumbled again, causing a very noticeable cry of anguish from a number of women in the crowd.

Jesus heard them and, despite his suffering, he raised his voice to the crowd saying, "Daughters of Jerusalem, do not weep for me; weep for yourselves and for your children. For the time will come when you will say, 'Blessed are the barren women, the wombs that never bore and the breasts that never nursed.' They will say to the mountains, 'Fall on us!' and to the hills, 'Cover us!' For if men do these things when the tree is green, what will happen when it is dry?"

I realized that he was quoting from the prophecies of Isaiah, and in particular, Hosea!

Bitter the cries of woe now, but nothing of the moment would compare with the wail of grief described in the book of Lamentations, written by our, "weeping prophet," Jeremiah, that prophesied the end result of this procession.

In a short twenty-seven years from now, our nation would cease to exist for more than nineteen hundred years!

CHAPTER 27

Golgotha

I HAVE EARLIER DESCRIBED the physical details of a crucifixion. And though we grimace at it's reading, believe me, those spikes reached deep into the psyche of every witness.

Needless to say, I personally had never witnessed a crucifixion before, although they were common in my lifetime. To be sure I had seen from a distance the bodies of its victims, after all, they were displayed on a hill!

This time however there was no escaping it. As an accuser I was required to be present for the execution.

So there we were: The Chief Priests with the more conspicuous members of the Sanhedrin, and of course a considerable number of the vengeful rabble crowd, although noticeably fewer than had demanded Jesus' crucifixion at Pilate's palace.

I guess it is one thing to wag the accusing finger, but quite another thing to stomach the travesty at the end of it. Apparently the fee for their cooperation did not include that of the usual professional mourners!

You must pardon my sarcasm! It's quite evident that I had not yet learned the art of forgiveness.

Before this day was out I would!

It might seem strange that there were so few present that had been the recipients of Jesus' loving ministry. Some had been physically healed from their infirmities. Some had received an exorcism, evermore released from the power of their demons. And regardless of their earthly needs, not one of them would ever deny the healing of their soul that they had received from the "Man of Galilee." Their healing was God's own proof of his love toward all who repent of their sins.

In all fairness, much of Jesus' ministry had been done in Galilee. The cost of travel to Jerusalem, and accommodation to boot, was beyond many of them on whom Jesus had shown such compassion, not to mention the inflated exchange rates for the required temple currency. Add to that the cost of their animal/bird sacrifices that had to be purchased there as well, and every excuse is justified.

But those present stood in silence, save for their quiet sobs, overwhelmed with a mixed bag of emotions. Anger at the injustice of it all! Remorse that they had not been present to defend him! Anguish at the thought of the cruelty they were witnessing! Confused as to why a loving God would allow such a travesty! Fearful to face a future now bereft of every hope of deliverance and salvation, for there was no longer anyone they could turn to for solace!

Somewhat obscured on the fringe of the crowd, were a few of us Pharisees who had objected to such criminal proceedings. We knew full well who were the criminals amid this crowd, and they weren't to be found on crosses!

To my mind, there was only one person present on Golgotha. No! I do not speak of Jesus this time. *I was that person!*

I am sure you agree that there are times when overwhelmed with the significance of the occasion we feel utterly alone even amid a large crowd. It may be our reluctance to be there. It may be feelings of guilt that we are there at all. It may be that we are central to the event, be it good or bad.

Deep within us, we know that this moment holds us at a crossroads where every decision will propel us into an unknown destiny!

That is where I stood now!

No matter my deepening appreciation for this common Jew. No matter my being convinced of his innocence. No matter my defense of him. All of it was thought and done in secret.

To this point I had made no public affirmation of my personal convictions concerning him. Once again we are confronted with the cornerstone of belief – public affirmation!

If I in the slightest believed Jesus was who he said he was, there certainly remained an obvious reluctance to forsake all and follow him.

In human costs the price was enormous! But along the yardstick of eternity it could not even find its place on the ruler.

I might doctrinally uphold the party's position of a resurrection to life beyond death, but you would never know it by the tight hold I had on earthly prestige and possessions. It must have, at some point in my religious life, occurred to me that my profession of religious convictions deserved a higher place in my soul than material riches. But when "push came to shove" convenience easily outweighed conviction.

And so there I stood on Golgotha's hill in abject misery, weighed down with guilt I had never known so keenly before, and in utter despair that I, a religious and political leader should be party to so criminal an act as was played out before me.

If it would please God in Heaven to forgive me, I could find no sense of it in my religion!

I could not know that in a very short time, from a cross, the first relief for my sorrow would come!

There were many others who at this very moment surely must have been as filled with guilt and remorse as I was, but they were conspicuous by their absence.

In fact, upon reflection, was not this particular execution fodder for a general uprising? Surely there could be expected a much larger contingent of soldiers beyond the execution party. I suspect they were on alert back at the barracks.

Above all, where were his disciples? There was only one at the foot of Jesus' cross in support of Mary the grieving mother. That was John.

Given the disgrace of their abandonment of Jesus at Gethsemane, and the fact that they were now marked men, I conclude that you and I are hardly justified in our own finger wagging!

Where they were at this moment is a secret best left to a more appropriate part of my tale.

But I see I am getting ahead of myself!

Upon arrival at the place of execution, the soldiers lost no time in getting the prisoners on their crosses, starting with the two thieves.

Now, I know that in your modern traditions the scene of the crucifixion sometimes shows the thieves bound with ropes, while Jesus is nailed to the cross, or other variations seemingly proffered to lessen the emotional impact of such a horrid portrayal.

But let me assure you there were no ropes, except those used to lift Jesus' cross into its anchor in the ground and raise each thief, already nailed to their cross-beam, into the appropriate position for lashing to the upright beam, after which their feet would be spiked to the cross.

The air shrieked with the cries of pain inflicted, reaching well beyond the perimeter of Golgotha, reminding those too timid to observe the scene visually that Roman justice was once again being administered.

When Jesus' turn came about, before he was fastened to his cross, the soldiers nailed a poster at the top of the upright beam that supposedly announced his crime. But this one seemed to be special. It was written in three languages, Aramaic, Latin and Greek. It read, "JESUS OF NAZARETH, THE KING OF THE JEWS."

The chief priests immediately caught Pilate's irony, and proceedings were delayed until a delegation went to Pilate and protested that there should be inserted after his name the words, "HE CLAIMED TO BE."

I learned later that Pilate gave them a curt sarcastic smile and said, "What I have written, I have written," and dismissed them without further argument.

Some would have you believe that Jesus was nailed to his cross without so much as a murmur. I assure you that, whether divine or no, he was totally and completely man with every nerve, sinew and bone of a human being.

No! It is too much to expect that he would receive heaven-sent relief, to the chagrin of the other two executed.

In fact, the prisoners were first offered a drink of wine mixed with myrrh, a very strong concoction intended to quickly produce a stupor that might help them bear the pain.

When Jesus took but a taste of it, he refused the offer.

There have been multiple paintings and films of the crucifixion, sufficient to lessen the pathos of our own emotions, caused by the account of such indignities as Jesus suffered. But I assure you that a Roman execution spared no detail of human abasement.

Believe me, his excruciation was no less than that of the other two!

The clothing removed was then distributed among the execution party according to their mutual agreement, with no regard for the wishes of next-of-kin that might be present.

In this case, the undergarment of Jesus was seamless, and being unwilling to destroy it, they decided by casting lots to determine its next owner.

I have often wondered what thoughts attended the man wearing the garment of one so noble as its former owner!

As he surveyed the crowd below him, Jesus noticed his grieving mother being supported on either side by his aunt Mary, wife of Cleopas. And there she was! Another Mary! Mary Magdalene, the recipient of perhaps the greatest work of exorcism ever performed by Jesus; The woman who had wiped Jesus' brow with his mother's handkerchief!

Just behind them he saw his beloved John, the only disciple in attendance.

To his mother he called out "Dear woman, here is your son," and to John he said, "Here is your mother."

But where was his family? His mother to be sure, but what of his four brothers, not to mention his sisters?

Now it was common knowledge among Jesus' entourage that some of his family members were not in favor of his ministry for reasons never made public. In fact, on one occasion, his mother and his brothers came together to the place where he was teaching. The crowds were so dense it was quite impossible for them to penetrate the human wall that latecomers encountered.

Whatever their business, it seemed urgent enough that they asked that a message be forwarded to Jesus as to their presence.

Whereupon Jesus had used the interruption as an opportunity to press home the point he was making concerning the predicament incurred by those who rejected his teachings.

"Who is my mother, and who are my brothers?" he asked, and pointing to his disciples he said, "Here are my mother and my brothers. For whoever does the will of my Father in Heaven is my brother and sister and mother."

I raise the point because human relationships can often interfere with the commitment one might make to a higher cause.

Jesus certainly taught that his teachings could precipitate strained relationships within one's household that might compromise the higher calling of one persuaded to follow him.

We must not conclude anything but that his family was concerned for his general welfare and even his safety, given the opposition he received from the Sanhedrin.

Mary, undoubtedly aware of her son's potential, had some understanding that his priorities underlined the very purpose for the divine nature of his birth.

It was to be understood that his siblings, born of her union with her husband Joseph, might have feelings of envy, especially given the claim of both her and Joseph to Jesus' immaculate conception, that was generally held by the religious authorities to be suspect, to say the very least.

Could one conclude other than that their absence at Golgotha signified a reluctance to accept his claims to divinity despite his ministry of miracles and the price he was paying for it?

I can, without effort, surmise their reluctance that Mary should attend her son's execution, the driving tortured love of a despairing mother winning the day.

In the ensuing annals of the Christian epistles there is but a terse mention of his brothers that possibly confirms their eventual conversion. His brother James did convert to Christianity, and rose to the position of Bishop of Jerusalem.

It surely is evident that Jesus did not teach any standards of commitment that he was unwilling to carry out.

"...Father, forgive them,..."

(Luke 23:34;)

CHAPTER 28

Forgiveness

And then it came!

Relief from my guilt that I had despaired of as I observed the hideous outcome of this "unforgivable crime," and my part in it!

Oh, what a tender scene! Oh what hope! Oh what victory! Oh what grace! As Jesus, amid the excruciating pain of his suffering, prayed aloud for us all, "Father, forgive them for they do not know what they are doing."

Surely, in the fading hours of his life, Jesus was epitomizing the totality of his teachings.

I recalled a day, when present on the mountainside, I, with other Pharisees, heard what was to become known as "The sermon on the Mount." It was the greatest lesson Jesus ever preached!

I can assure you it brought, to us teachers of the Law of Moses, much consternation when he deliberately attacked the Talmud yet again.

He said, "You have heard that it was said, 'Love your neighbor and hate your enemy.' But I tell you: Love your enemies and pray for those who persecute you, that you may be sons of your Father in heaven."

Now he was practicing what he had preached!

I reflect again!

A man? Yes truly flesh and blood! I know, because I saw it ripped apart and the blood flowing.

Only three years into the ministry, begun at thirty years of age as set by our own traditions. A ministry filled with the greatest revelation of God then, now, or ever to be afforded to man through time immemorial.

And we had snatched it away!

Talk about unfairness! Talk about a God of wrath! Yet there he was upon a cross asking God to forgive us, who had hung him there thinking we did God a service!

Yes! Exclamation after exclamation! I make no apology for it.

It was apparent to me that Jesus had a totally different concept of God than we did.

He was at this very moment imbued with a presence of the divine that was unknown and unfathomable to us religious leaders.

That a man being unjustly executed for crimes he never committed should forgive his executioners? Could it be that in these excruciating circumstances he had found a source of love that was yet unknown to us?

I could not know it now, but I would soon learn that *God is love*!

But if God is love, then how much more calloused could our response have been?

No! It was not enough just to crucify Jesus and leave him alone!

The taunting of Jesus was a downright aggravation to me.

Did the two thieves receive any ridicule the whole time?

No! But Jesus got it from all sides!

The rabble crowd was the most boisterous, spurred on by the Chief Priest who was equal in his verbal abuse, but too arrogant to lower himself to public outcry. He set the pace, and, I might sadly add, the majority of the Sanhedrin joined in.

"He saved others," they said, "but he can't save himself! He's the King of Israel! Let him come down now from the cross and we will believe in him. He trusts in God. Let God rescue him now if he wants him, for he said, 'I am the Son of God.'"

Did they not think God could do it? They need only ask those who had tried to arrest him!

This gave courage to the Roman soldiers to join in the mockery. They had no depth of knowledge or understanding of Jewish beliefs and practices, but they parroted the ridicule, if for no other reason than to give themselves some sense of relief from having executed a man so obviously more noble than his accusers.

The greater one's unrequited guilt, the greater bravado it will always take to hide it.

I noted with some amazement that the Roman Centurion of the detachment did not join in with his troops. Indeed he seemed aloof from his men, as though he was pondering some deeper nuance of the scene.

Then, amid the din, there came about two extraordinary incidents.

The first!

One of the thieves joined in the ridicule, but with a far more personal and urgent agenda: "Aren't you the Christ? Save yourself and us!"

Oh I have no doubt that his cry came from the depth of his own despair that his life was ebbing away to where and what he did not know, thus perhaps granting him some credibility for his actions. If there was a whist of a chance that what Jesus claimed was true, then in God's name get him to do it now!

His pitiable cries were suddenly drowned out by a louder voice, though filled with the same agonies as the first.

"Don't you fear God," it said, "since you are under the same sentence?" So spoke the other thief. "We are punished justly, for we are getting what our deeds deserve. But this man has done nothing wrong," he continued.

This was phenomenal! That one, himself fully guilty of the crimes for which he bore his punishment, should publicly acknowledge his wrongdoing, and then make an outright statement of faith in Jesus as the Son of God. In a voice strong enough for all to hear, he said, "Jesus, remember me when you come into your kingdom."

Oh! To this day his confession strikes enormous incredulity into my heart for the hypocrisy of our religious pomposity. That we leaders of Israel should have wagged our heads, as this lowly suffering human being bowed his! What insensitivity!

And then the second wonder!

That this lowly thief should be the very first soul to enter the Kingdom of God on this first day of grace! How he must have thrilled to the words, "I tell you the truth, today you will be with me in paradise."

Are these not the words that every man should long to hear, ere he faces the judgment bar of God?

I knew then that I was witness to the greatest demonstration of unconditional love that man could ever hope to see!

CHAPTER 29

The Real Price

Now I MAKE no digression to bring some understanding to the Jewish day calendar. It is very helpful in understanding the duration of Jesus' suffering in relationship to the impending Passover that was by now just hours away.

The commencement of our day began at sunset. The day was then divided into two major divisions of twelve hours each – twelve night hours – and twelve daylight hours. Each of these two divisions was then divided into four watches of three hours each.

The arrest of Jesus, having taken place in the darker hours, meant that the arrest, trial and procession to Golgotha had absorbed approximately six of those night hours and the first watch (three hours) of daylight.

It meant that Jesus had been crucified at midday, referred to by John Mark in his Gospel as the third hour. All that I have already described to you of the crucifixion, took place within that third watch.

Still he would suffer in silence for almost another three hours.

It was at the sixth hour that there was a decided change in the weather.

Heavy dark storm clouds moved in from the east completely blocking out the sun, creating an eerie blackness as if in the midnight hour. The wind increased dramatically convincing us all of an impending storm, from the like of which we had best be seeking shelter.

We were suddenly transfixed by the wailing gut-wrenching cry of Jesus calling out to his god.

Yes! I said, "his god," because I tell you right now, we accusers certainly had no sense of a righteous god in any of this. Remember! We had dared that if he was the Christ, let the god of heaven come and rescue him.

But listen to his words. "*My* God, *my* God, why have you forsaken me?"

Though it was evident to me that he thought himself to be abandoned by God, it was not a cry of anger. It seemed rather the words reflected an agony of spirit far beyond the physical pain inflicted by the cross.

They seemed to indicate a relationship, perhaps even a fellowship with God that unexpectedly he had suddenly lost.

It was one thing to lay down one's life for whatever benefit to others. But why would such an act suddenly obliterate all sense of justification for the sacrifice?

We did not understand it. In fact it elicited a false sense of justification to his accusers, that finally this imposter now suffered the consequences of his own delusions.

But there was one in the crowd who sensed that here was no apostasy, no unbelief!

Had he not told me, just two nights before, that it was necessary that he, the "Son of Man" as he called himself, must be lifted up? And I had known then, with horror, that it would be a cross.

How could I possibly misconstrue his words, just spoken, to be anything but the agony of soul he now bore on that cross for *my* sins, let alone all mankind?

In consequence, God had turned away his face from the object of sin!

Somehow I knew in my heart that here, on this cross, was payment in full for the apostasy of his accusers, of his nation, indeed of all mankind! Jesus of Nazareth had somehow been made sin for us!

It mattered not if I alone had been the object of redemption that fateful day. It would have changed nothing – except for the tears of penitence that now stained the face of a thoroughly chastened Pharisee whose ecclesiastical robes hung as filthy rags upon my back!

The storm was fast gathering momentum and it seemed that some intervention should be made to hasten the death and removal of these three suffering victims, that usually involved the breaking of the legs, thus removing any support for the body weight, resulting in swift suffocation.

But Jesus brought matters to a standstill when soon after his lamenting cry he added, "I thirst."

We later equated this statement with the fulfillment of the prophecy of King David, "They put gall in my food and gave me vinegar for my thirst."

Even on the brink of death Jesus obviously had presence of mind to assure the completion of prophecy concerning his demise.

Somehow a few overzealous Pharisees thought that he was calling for Elijah, and intentionally added another dimension to their mockery. This prophet had been propelled bodily into heaven without tasting death. If Jesus were a prophet of God, surely God would release him from imminent death in the same miraculous manner.

Although surely ignorant of the prophetic significance of his actions, one of them lifted to Jesus lips, by means of a pole, a sponge soaked with wine vinegar, a putrid concoction of soured wine, and said, "Now leave him alone. Let's see if Elijah comes to take him down."

I saw no evidence that Jesus did other than taste this prohibited drink, and as though satisfied that there was nothing more required of him he said, "it is finished."

His reference was not to the drink offered. It was telling us, and his Heavenly Father that the whole purpose of his coming to this earth was now completed. Once more he addressed his God with a loud cry. "Father, into your hands I commit my spirit."

As Doctor Luke later so gracefully wrote it, "When he had said this, he breathed his last."

It was the last moment ever that the priesthood of our religion, and the Sanhedrin, would ever exercise control of the spiritual destiny of our nation!

In an immeasurable instant the storm broke with a cataclysmic roar of lightning and thunder that brought every human being present to their knees if not their backsides.

Unceremoniously we reeled like drunken sailors as a devastating earthquake tore open the ground, unearthed the graves in the cemetery, toppled houses, cracked and damaged some of the city walls, and shook the temple to its foundations.

Still, the crosses stood erect as though supernaturally protected from the devastation that lay all around them.

The Centurion in charge of the execution, standing in front of Jesus and hearing his cry, obviously seeing something in the death of Jesus that we had not witnessed, knelt on bended knees and cried out, "Surely this man was the Son of God!"

His utterance would not be the only evidence to the truth that had been revealed to him!

One of the priests came running in a panic from the direction of the temple exclaiming "The Temple! The Temple! Oh the Holy of Holies in the Temple!"

Unable to quiet the man, the High Priest asked what news he had concerning its condition. In words loud enough for all to hear he babbled, "The curtain! The curtain! It's destroyed, ripped in half from the top to the bottom *and God's not there!* He's always been there hasn't he? The High Priests have always told us so! Why tomorrow Caiaphas you are to go behind it to offer up sins for the people for the past year are you not? Now whatever shall we do?"

The Chief Priest, the Sanhedrin and most of the crowd beat a hasty retreat to the Temple.

But there was one, and as it turned out, two members of the Sanhedrin who did not leave the cross!

To the consternation of the total city populace, many people ran hither and yon through the streets in absolute panic claiming that their resurrected relatives, friends and associates had risen from the graves and had confronted them!

I cannot adequately explain why I could not leave, if not for affairs at the Temple, at least to assure the safety of my family and the condition of my home.

As concerned as I would normally be at such devastating news, somehow I no longer seemed to care.

Then he came and stood beside me! It was Joseph of Arimathea.

The tears were streaming down his face in company with mine as we both looked into the eyes of the other and knew that this Jesus had won our hearts.

Joseph told me of his concern that the body of Jesus would be unceremoniously buried in the potters' field, purchased by the Sanhedrin with the thirty pieces of silver Judas had cast on the floor before the Chief Priest, evidently in remorse for his act of betrayal.

This was simply unthinkable to Joseph!

We agreed he would quickly and privately approach Pilate for permission to take charge of the body of Jesus for decent burial. He would use a brand new tomb, hued from solid rock and as yet unused, located in the garden of his estate.

He left immediately, asking that I seek permission of Mary his mother who, with John, still remained at the cross.

The Centurion, somewhat recovered from his unexpected act of devotion, mercifully had ordered his detail to break the legs of the two thieves, and prepared to do the same for Jesus.

Seeing that he was in all likelihood dead, he forbade the soldiers to touch him, and he personally cast a spear into Jesus' side. The resulting flow of blood and water, neither contaminated by the other, assured the fact.

Though Jesus himself could not affect this fulfillment of prophecy, almighty God had used this once pagan soldier to do so as his first Christian act of love!

As I observed this, I remembered the words of the psalmist, "… he protects all his bones, not one of them will be broken."

Pilate, evidently still skittish about the outcome of his day, was skeptical of Joseph's news that Jesus was now dead. He sent a soldier to summon the Centurion, and having confirmed that Jesus was dead, ordered him to give the body to Joseph.

As quickly as it had appeared the storm abated; As though God himself had made a statement and then turned his back on us.

And he had!

"...Destroy this temple, and I will raise it again in three days."

(John 2:19;)

CHAPTER 30

True Colors

THE CENTURION NODDED to Joseph, indicating that we should take the women away from their vigil at the base of the cross. John suggested to them that they might wish to leave the soldiers to their work, hoping that they could be saved from further anguish.

Despite their compliance, I am certain that Mary's gaze never left the presence of her son!

The soldiers then busied themselves removing the bodies of the two thieves. When it came to Jesus, the Centurion waved them off, as he personally, ever so tenderly, with the tears flowing, loosed the feet from their fetter, and climbing the ladder, released the arms of Jesus from the cross beam and ever so carefully lowered him into the waiting arms of his troops.

He then conferred with Joseph, and under his direction they carried the body of Jesus to the tomb, followed closely by John, with Mary, Jesus' mother. The other Mary - wife of Joses, Mary Magdalene, and myself completed the procession.

The women were more than satisfied with this beautiful sepulcher, and they were overwhelmed with gratitude, at the kindness of Joseph of Arimathea.

But now, with the abating of the storm, no time must be wasted in preparing the body for the grave.

With Joseph's agreement I hastily returned to the city and went straight to a seller of myrrh and aloes, and purchased seventy-five pounds of it, plus a quantity of strips of linen that, in my company, his attendants delivered to the tomb. These would be used for an external embalming of the body that the women would perform as soon as the Passover day was ended.

The women stood to one side as we men, aided by the soldiers and some of Joseph's household servants, rolled a huge circular rock across the entrance. It had been carefully selected and tooled to prevent any entry of man or beast.

The soldiers then left us to our grief, but I saw the Centurion privately address Jesus' mother, before he left, undoubtedly extending his condolences, and surely to ask her forgiveness for his part in the execution, and I have no doubt, to confess his new-born faith in her son as the divine Son of God.

Then the rest of us prepared to return, each to our own home, but not before these resolute women had arranged to meet at the tomb on Sunday morning, well before the light of day, to perform their aforementioned duties.

Mary, the mother of Jesus, left us safely and lovingly, supported on the arm of John, her new beloved son.

They were undoubtedly headed for the place where the other disciples were now safely ensconced.

I was much relieved and yes, apologetic to my wife that I arrived home so late, to find that, apart from toppled pottery and curios, the house was not damaged. That was more than I could say for other lesser-constructed homes throughout the city.

She sensed that I had come through my own epiphany at that cross, and though in an hour or so I would perform the male rite of the Passover meal, she had already tidied up the quake-induced mess and laid out a resplendent table for the most sacred ceremonial meal of the year.

There was time for me to confidentially tell of the events at the crucifixion, minus the gory details, emphasizing the amazing spirituality of the occasion.

She was most empathetic to my new experience, although still in need of further enlightenment. But I could sense a great depth of understanding within her very soul that suggested to me, that since her earlier confession that she believed Jesus was the Messiah, she now knew that his cross somehow held a deeper significance for her soul.

It was abundantly clear to me that we would this night sit at our feast with a deeper sense of cleansing than just another year of forgiveness would afford.

Neither then nor now, can I even imagine what was transpiring at the Temple!

The Chief Priest and all of the Sanhedrin, but for Josephus and I, were by now busily examining the temple building for any damage. I can confirm from my later visits that it had survived the earthquake without damage save for the veil.

You might correctly conjecture that the view of the Holy Place was prohibited to all but the Levitical Priests appointed to its function, but let me tell you, all holy ordinance had given way to utter chaos as Priest, Pharisee, Sadducee and Sanhedrin stood together aghast at the forbidden scene of judgment that had fallen upon us all.

We are not to assume that the temple stood unscathed by reason of its magnificent structure, as though it defied man or God to destroy it. In less than thirty years from now that building would forever lie in stark ruin, not one stone upon another, the victim of Roman retribution against the impending national uprising that would destroy our nation, in fulfillment of the very prophecy Jesus had made to his disciples just a few days before he was arrested.

But I digress!

The veil was sixty feet high and four inches thick (by your measurements) and its woven materials so strong that even a team of horses pulling on each side could not have ripped it an inch apart, much less from top to bottom!

There was no damage to the pillars and walls upon which the veil was hung. Yet this curtain, that separated the Holy of Holies from the Holy Place and the rest of the Temple, hung limp in two parts, without sign of burning, its tear the more damaged at the top, but nonetheless complete through to the bottom, exposing to all priests on duty in the Holy Place, the Ark of the Covenant, from which they fled in consummate panic.

This very night God was to have presented himself to the High Priest in the pillar of cloud between the cherubim, and grant absolution of sins to all Jews for another year.

One can only imagine the heightened anticipation of Caiaphas as the hour approached for him to enter the Holy of Holies behind the veil and make penitential intercession for his own sins and the sins of the people, an honor that came but once in a lifetime. For Caiaphas it would never be!

There would be no sacrifices and High Priestly prayers made this night!

There was no need! It was true! God was not there!

CHAPTER 31

Revenge

THE FURY OF Caiaphas is beyond description, save to say that his pathos became fuel for his livid anger, and his anger into raging lust for revenge!

If it had not been for the sanctimonious decorum of his holy office expected of him, I conjecture that he might well have personally involved himself in the removal of Jesus' body from the cross for the shear satisfaction of committing it to the adjacent garbage dump.

Surely nothing short of his punishment of Joseph and I would satisfy his vengeance, once he learned that we had taken charge of Jesus' body for burial, and with the permission of Pilate at that.

Even more offensive to him would be the use of Joseph's garden sepulcher for the purpose.

Fortunately for me, unaware of Joseph's fate, I was nowhere in sight when the High Priest's own detachment of Roman Guards (the same that had arrested Jesus in the garden) were dispatched to take Joseph into custody.

The Passover night now almost upon us, they put Joseph into a windowless shed on his own property, locked the only door with a strong lock, and placed a guard at the entrance.

I presume, that for the same reason, they did not bother me at home. There would be plenty of time to deal with both delinquent Pharisees after Passover!

The incarceration of Joseph must have heightened the concern of Caiaphas for the security of the tomb.

I presume, at the utter annoyance of Pilate, who by now was likely well into his evening meal, and already huffed by the earlier interruption of his breakfast, Caiaphas, personally, made an urgent request to Pilate that he order the dispatch of some of the soldiers of his supreme guard to the garden tomb to secure it, with the affixing of the Governor's seal upon the entrance.

His request was based on the prophecy of Jesus that he would be resurrected on the third day of his demise.

He thought it likely that his disciples would come to the tomb and steal the body and declare that Jesus had risen from the dead, in his opinion exacerbating the first deception of Jesus' claim to be the Son of God!

What of my Passover?

Both my wife and I were perhaps somewhat chagrined at my fulfilling the traditional role of priest as I presided at our own feast. We both knew that my days as a member of the Sanhedrin were likely now ended. In fact we were somewhat unnerved at the thought of the knock on our door that would come probably at the very commencement of the following day at the next sunset, to propel me to whatever fate awaited me.

But this was a time for solemnity and silence as with our assembled family we said the prayers of confession and recited yet again the ancient deliverance of Israel from Egyptian bondage, feasting upon the sacrificial lamb to its total consumption. Then jubilation! The giving of gifts! The celebration of another new year! And not in the least the warmth and love of family, truly the greatest blessing one could receive from our Creator God.

Of course these festivities had proceeded all through the night. As daylight broke, our married children and their families made their way home. Those still at home contented themselves with their gifts and all the excitement of the continued holiday that lasted for seven days.

Company gone and the house tidied, my wife and I had opportunity to reflect on the circumstances that had befallen us over these past days of the Jesus episode.

We most certainly anticipated retribution for my part in coming to Jesus' defense and participation in his burial. But of greater importance was why I had involved myself in the first place.

No, I was not second-guessing myself! And don't think for a moment that I was displaying bravado natural to my instincts.

It was all his doing! Jesus I mean!

I will not repeat myself with the intimate details I have already written in this book, suffice to say that, consciously, even if not fully understood, I was being propelled by uncontrollable circumstances that I now know were intentionally sculpted to my soul's need.

I must, however, be willing to trust my God to lead me into new revelation and the resolve of soul issues that had eluded me throughout my religious life. The sincerity of my belief system and my position in the religious hierarchy of our nation were just not a part of this equation.

I know you are anxious to ask if at this point I was converted to Jesus Christ. In fact you have probably made this conclusion.

I confess to some monumental issues that held me in spiritual limbo between my religious disciplines and a soul-gripping conviction that Jesus was truly the Son of God, our Messiah; Yes! Even my Savior!

Such a confession was yet to be supremely tested by the subsequent challenges that lay before me, lest you should determine that my present state was some whim born of the enormous emotional rollercoaster these days had inflicted upon me.

Those challenges were very real, even to the point of ominous!

Oh, I have shared earlier in my story some of the more obvious material and social issues that even the slightest involvement with Jesus might impact. But now, the price tag of such a relationship loomed very large, even to the potential forfeiting of my life, resulting in immeasurable consequences that would be inflicted upon my wife and family.

To whom could they turn for consummate support if my life was taken, indeed if even they themselves were spared?

Was it fair that our children should bear the stigma born of the incomprehensible actions of their father, or even perhaps, both parents?

And where did all this lead?

What would be the end-result?

Jesus was now dead! His disciples in hiding! Caiaphas on the warpath! Would-be converts left with only whimsical memories of a moment of hope!

Already it was too late! I had gone too far, devastated by the weight of raw power and sinister hatred unleashed from within the very bowels of a religion that boasted us Jews to be the chosen people of God!

And then came the knock on our door!

"Anyone who loves his father or mother more than me is not worthy of me;…"

(Matthew 10:37;)

CHAPTER 32

A New Journey

To the utter relief of my wife and I, it was John standing at the door.

I, unceremoniously, pulled him inside!

It was wise of him to have come under cover of darkness, and obvious that he had taken every precaution to disguise his appearance.

Whatever possessed him to leave the confines of their secret hiding place I do not know, except that he had related to the other disciples the sympathies of Joseph and I toward Jesus and the women, explaining our part in his burial.

They had apparently agreed that I should be informed of the news they had received from the sympathetic owner of the place where they were staying, of Joseph's arrest and subsequent escape from custody!

We of course were ecstatic at the news, but utterly bewildered when they informed us that, without any means of exit, when the guards opened the door of the thoroughly secured shed he was not there, and nowhere to be found.

There was apparently some surreptitious power at work here although never to be admitted by his captors.

I could only surmise the anger of Caiaphas and the embarrassment of the Roman Guard. Would heads roll, or more likely the guards be bribed? It was likely we would never know.

Where was Joseph? We would have to wait for the answers to these questions.

Meanwhile, John thought it advisable that my wife and I, and whatever family necessary, should make a hasty retreat from Jerusalem. As quickly as possible, he would get to us any information and instructions necessary to our safety.

Understandably, it was impossible that he should invite us to accompany him to his current sanctuary, given the need for security and the lack of trust of myself on the part of the others.

With fond wishes for our safety, John then left our premises.

It was obviously time for us to share our confidences with the married sons and daughters and those at home, trusting that despite whatever disappointments and misgivings they might have for my actions, they would remain loyal to their parents and aid in whatever deceptions necessary to conceal our whereabouts.

I confess my gratitude for my immense wealth that would facilitate whatever measures we deemed necessary for our safety.

There were two circumstances that aided our escape from Jerusalem!

The present religious holiday would tend to deter any attempt to track us down, and the highways would be busy with pilgrims returning to their homes following the celebrations. Also it was quite common for folks to make tracks to warmer climes at this time of the year. We need not go to our own summer villas. We could quite afford to stay in the finest accommodations available in any number of neighboring countries.

Before the day was far spent we were on our way to our "vacation," destination unknown! No! You are not to know that either!

Now, you are likely familiar with the details of the account of Jesus' resurrection from the dead, contained in the New Testament Gospels of The Holy Bible.

Not having been present in Jerusalem during those exciting days, for reasons just revealed, I am not in a position, if so inclined, to add any details here.

I can attest to the truth of those accounts, given that in the course of our journey we happened upon Joseph in his hometown of Arimathea in Galilee.

When we arrived there the whole region was abuzz with news of Jesus' resurrection.

Jesus, now very much alive, had appeared, first to the women who had gone to the tomb to further anoint his body, and then to the disciples and their entourage sequestered in their hiding place.

He had ordered that they return to Galilee where he would meet with them by the same supernatural means with which he had first revealed himself raised from the dead.

Galilee was home base for all the disciples, and had been the dominant area of most of Jesus' ministry.

John assured the other disciples of Joseph's sympathy with their cause, and they had sought him out, perhaps for some influential protection, as much as to commiserate over their traumatic experiences.

Joseph said that it was only natural that they, being fishermen, would try their hand at their old trade until Jesus should appear to give them further instructions. So they had returned to their boats that they had left in the care of others, three years before.

Evidently, it was while the disciples were fishing, that Jesus met up with them, under the same circumstances they had encountered when he first asked them to be his disciples; No fish!

Obviously amused, Joseph told how he had been informed that Jesus had appeared on the shore within calling distance of the boat, but not sufficiently close for them to identify him.

As per the time before, Jesus asked them if they had caught any fish, and when they said "No," he suggested they throw their nets over the other side of the boat. With nothing to lose they did it, and "ditto" – the net was full of fish so that it was near the breaking point, just like the first time!

During our visit together Joseph told me about his adventures with Caiaphas.

By his own account, sometime through the night, an angel had appeared to him and whisked him away, through sealed walls, in complete deception of the guards who defended their own fidelity and ignorance of what had happened.

Much amused, Joseph said it was later noted that the composite of the temple guard seemed to change dramatically, and that the original group seemed to have come upon much improved circumstances.

But I must get on with my story!

The angel had deposited Joseph safely in his own house in Arimathea, telling him that Jesus had risen from the dead.

He told me that Jesus had personally appeared to him, proving his authenticity by the same wounds he had displayed to his disciples, after he had first entered their hiding place right through locked doors.

Jesus had told Joseph that he would meet with his disciples here in Galilee, during which he would give them final instructions.

We discussed my situation at length, and though there could be no guarantees, Joseph thought the supernatural events now in play should give Caiaphas sufficient caution in any discipline he might be tempted to inflict upon me.

He even suggested that my extreme wealth might play a part in my defense, not to suggest a bribe, but to recognize the broad influence I carried in the community from which the temple treasury amply benefited.

In fact Joseph was even now preparing to return to Jerusalem, having made plans with three officials from his local synagogue to precede him to announce they had found him, and to tell Caiaphas of the supernatural circumstances of his escape.

These men were of no mean stature in the hierarchy of the synagogue. Phinees was the presiding priest and Addas a noted teacher in the local Hebrew school. Aggaeus the Levite was in charge of the preparations for all the ceremonial rites of worship in the synagogue.

Of greatest importance was the fact that these three men had personally witnessed the presence of Jesus in company with his disciples as they approached the mountainside where he had arranged to take them.

It was the very mountain from which Jesus, Peter, James and John had descended following their meeting with Moses and Elijah, during which Jesus had been supernaturally transfigured into the same eternal state he had enjoyed in the presence of his Father God, prior to his immaculate conception and human birth.

This fact, at the instruction of Jesus, not to be revealed until after his death and resurrection, was forever memorialized by Jesus' healing of the young boy consumed with massive epileptic seizures, that had defied the earlier attempts of the other nine disciples.

These men further related to Joseph and I that they had learned that Jesus and his disciples would be traveling back to the vicinity of Jerusalem, presumably to the same place where they had sought sanctuary during his trial and crucifixion.

Joseph strongly cautioned us that no word of Jesus' return to Jerusalem must be leaked.

I was to learn later that in his conversations with Jesus, he had been told of his impending supernatural ascension into Heaven, the location of which must for the time remain secret.

Joseph suggested that I return with these leaders of the Synagogue to affirm their story. He thought this would increase the chances of a more amicable conclusion to my flight from Jerusalem.

Joseph was adamant that his return to Jerusalem would be voluntary, and only at the invitation of Caiaphas. There was no way he was going to let this tyrant hold court over him.

Caiaphas would have to acquiesce to the evidence of Jesus' resurrection, and his messianic claims, or Joseph could no longer support the unique authority of the High Priest.

After all, Joseph had already seen, and conversed, with the *risen* Christ!

Our departure was enriched by the warmth and respect that comes only between men of like conviction, and we parted amid a strange peace born of conjugal faith and the promise of supporting prayer.

It was with a pleasant calm that I breathed in the final aromas of the Sea of Galilee as a gentle wind swept inland to refresh my body and my spirit!

"You diligently study the Scriptures because you think that by them you possess eternal life..."

(John 5:39;)

CHAPTER 33

Head On

I ASSURE YOU THAT my appearance before Caiaphas was not met with the slightest courtesy between us.

Joseph was right! Caiaphas and the Sanhedrin were far too busy dealing with the repairs of the damaged temple. They certainly had no time, for the moment, to be concerned with this "traitorous Pharisee."

Many now believed the torn veil was the supernatural evidence of God's anger for our part in the crucifixion of Jesus.

On top of that, Jesus' body had disappeared from the tomb! Many believed this to be his bodily resurrection from the dead, bringing total incredulity to the claims of the High priest that his disciples had stolen the body from the tomb.

Caiaphas had, reportedly, given an enormous bribe to the soldiers of the Roman Imperial Guard to buy their deception concerning Jesus' resurrection from the dead. He had promised them his personal intervention with Pilate, should any of the details of their botched sentry watch come to his attention.

When I heard that, I cringed to think how Caiaphas could care less that they might be court-martialed and consequently executed! That would certainly provide an even more convenient protection for his falsehood.

Now he had a similar problem with the supernatural escape of Joseph, attested to by the three witnesses who had personally seen him at his home in Arimathea.

But here's the clincher!

They had also seen Jesus of Nazareth in conference with his delinquent disciples in Galilee!

What was he to do, short of calling them all liars? Which he did, even though they swore to the truth by the sacred name of Father Abraham who was the highest authority in whose name an oath could be made by a Jew.

Not satisfied with this, he had each of the three witnesses before him separately, hoping to find some inconsistency one from the other in their individual story.

It was obviously time for me to step forward in their defense!

Caiaphas belligerently and publicly condemned me to the same wrath of God, pursuant to the divine judgment he wished upon all who contradicted his own account of these monumental happenings.

Nevertheless he gave me the floor!

I conceded that I had not personally seen Jesus in Galilee, but that I most certainly had seen Joseph alive and well in his own home.

I related Joseph's personal account of his escape from captivity in the details he had shared with me.

My account that Jesus had appeared to Joseph in person, was attested to by the three witnesses

I have since concluded that it was the continued influence of the Holy Spirit upon me, similar to the soul stirring I had received throughout this drama that brought to mind a plan to test the validity of Jesus' resurrection.

The Spirit prompted me to remind Caiaphas of the supernatural intervention that God had brought to the prophet Elijah when he was personally conveyed to Heaven in the fiery chariot.

Elisha his servant, now bedewed with a double portion of his master's spirit, miraculously crossed back through the parted waters of the Jordan River, in similar fashion as Elijah had conducted them both to the opposite side.

I reminded him that the witnesses to Elisha's crossing were not willing to believe he was successor to Elijah until a thorough search for his master was made throughout the region.

To this Elisha had agreed, and only when they found no trace of Elijah after three days' search, did they accept his divine appointment as God's new prophet.

Caiaphas knew he was cornered!

Although he was disinclined to accept any word of mine, my next suggestion received overwhelming support by the Sanhedrin, and Caiaphas conceded to their wishes.

I proposed that we launch a major search for the person of Jesus throughout all Judea, and failing our capture of him, we would conclude that he indeed was the Divine Son of God, now taken into the presence of God the Creator!

The claims of Jesus would then be accepted, his disciples exonerated, and the temple worship modified to accommodate their witness!

I knew those seeking to discredit him would not find Jesus, and as expected, they returned empty-handed.

True to course, Caiaphas and the Sanhedrin reneged on their agreement, and refused to believe the clear evidence of Jesus' resurrection.

His blatant denial brought absolute exposure to his religious façade. High Priest or whatever! He might pretend to represent the greatest religion ever founded among men. But, he certainly did not represent the God his religion was meant to portray!

Now his attention turned to Joseph.

Caiaphas sent a delegation from the Sanhedrin to accompany the three witnesses back to Arimathea.

They were to deliver a letter from Caiaphas conveying his greeting, and requesting that Joseph return to Jerusalem to give personal account of his escape experience, and his alleged meeting with Jesus and his disciples.

His personal safety was assured, and the promise of accommodation given.

In fact I had told Caiaphas that my wife and I would be happy to host Joseph during his stay in Jerusalem. He would never be allowed to stay in his Jerusalem house for fear of further escape, and the adoring public would never tolerate another house arrest.

I was quick to remind them that a promise of peace and safety were not enough for Joseph. I related Joseph's position as he had told me, that beginning with Caiaphas, and including every member of the Sanhedrin, except myself, they were to express to him that they had wrongfully incarcerated him and ask his forgiveness.

You can well understand the reluctance of the High Priest to so lower himself, but confirmed by the three officials from Arimathea, that nothing less would prompt Joseph to return, they put such terms of confession in their letter, and sent the delegation on its way.

Joseph accepted the letter with his usual grace and hosted the delegates in his own home overnight, commencing his return in their company the following morning.

You can well understand that the details of his episode with Caiaphas and his remarkable escape from custody were now public knowledge.

As the noteworthy delegation approached the city Joseph was easily recognized by onlookers. In no time there began an increasing swell of praise and adoration.

This brought heightened caution to Caiaphas that he should avoid displaying any vehemence toward Joseph such as he had shown me.

The entire Sanhedrin accompanied Joseph to my house where my wife and I had prepared a sumptuous banquet for them all, with our guest seated at the place of honor. High Priests or no, Caiaphas and Annas would have to content themselves with being seated on either side of Joseph, with the remaining Sanhedrin members seated in positions usual to the regular business sessions.

I must say, my wife had simply outdone herself in the preparations, even to a separate but lavish spread for the wives who accompanied their elite husbands.

I can truly attest that the whole evening reflected the gracious times once experienced when our nation was not under its current distress. Even Caiaphas seemed to genuinely enjoy himself.

The evening celebrations concluded, all of our guests except Joseph departed, allowing my household staff the time to rearrange the banquet hall into a more formal setting for a business session of the Sanhedrin that would meet in my house the next day.

The hour being somewhat late, and given Joseph's lengthy trip to the city, he and I had some brief discussion concerning the forthcoming meeting, and he retired to his bed.

I confess that my wife and I, despite our strenuous hosting, slept rather fitfully!

I should explain that the meetings of the Sanhedrin were normally held in the Temple. But given the nature of our business and the repairs ongoing in the building to resolve the crisis within the Holy of Holies, it seemed appropriate that I offer my home as the meeting place.

I know, I can read your mind! You have already deducted that such a gesture could do no harm to the extremely tedious relations between the High Priest and myself! Yes! That thought had crossed my mind too!

But then too, the venue also provided added security for Joseph, both from gaping spectators common to our regular meetings, and from any untoward hostility that might yet raise its head within the Sanhedrin. We both knew that Caiaphas had not "rolled over" despite his knowledge of our position concerning Jesus!

Protocol was observed despite the change of locale, and as host I was afforded the first words of introduction to the agenda.

COME WITH THE WIND – NICODEMUS TELLS HIS STORY

To my mind there was no need of speechmaking, but for the sake of public record I spoke to Joseph directly, announcing the purpose of this particular session of the Sanhedrin. I invited him to address us concerning his imprisonment, escape and succeeding circumstances.

His position not to be ignored, Caiaphas demanded of Joseph that the truth of his account be attested to by the most stringent of oaths available to our customs.

Whereupon Joseph took the floor and in a most humble manner that enhanced his prestigious persona, he related the details of his escape that I have already covered in my story.

However we were not prepared for what happened next!

Upon his declaration that Jesus had indeed risen from the tomb, every man present, save for Joseph and myself, were overcome by a superhuman presence evading the whole room that caused them to temporarily swoon uncontrollably, some in their chairs as if in a faint, and others unceremoniously strewn on the floor.

Joseph and I both knew that the Holy Spirit of God had intervened on our behalf, strengthening the truth of our witness.

Regaining consciousness, there was much fright among them, and Joseph and I, beginning with Caiaphas, very gently helped them to regain their seating.

Clearly the meeting had progressed far past the issue of blame, be it the Sanhedrin, Caiaphas, Joseph or myself. Jesus had now become the center of focus.

The Sanhedrin thought it would be appropriate to call into counsel a noteworthy priest named Levi, from his duties at the temple.

He was well versed in the history of our nation both ancient and contemporary, and most importantly, he had witnessed the details of the presentation of Jesus at the temple by his parents. He recited word-for-word the blessing of Simeon affirming Jesus as the Messiah.

When challenged as to the source of his knowledge, it turned out Levi had been a student under the venerable Simeon, who had freely declared to his contemporaries, including his students, that he had personally seen and blessed the infant Jesus as the long awaited savior of Israel.

Surely Caiaphas would have to agree! He was now without excuse.

Not so!

In the face of overwhelming evidence the demons of ambition and pride were about to expose themselves!

As the discussion continued, the many precedents of the law were examined and Caiaphas took hold of the phrase, "Cursed is he who hangs on a tree."

He expected that this applied to Jesus so that he could not be considered the legitimate Messiah, given that his resurrection was, in Caiaphas' opinion still suspect.

Joseph remonstrated against Caiaphas, saying, if Jesus did not rise again from the dead, then what explanation could be given for the rising of many from their graves and their appearing to many in the city following the earthquake?

He made reference to the two sons of Simeon, the one who had blessed Jesus as a babe in this same temple in Jerusalem where the veil had been torn in two. These two men, Karinus and Leucius by name, had died and the total Sanhedrin had attended their burial.

First, the bombshell!

He told us that both men had indeed risen from their graves and even now were in Arimathea where in self-appointed seclusion they worshipped Jesus as their Messiah.

Now, the challenge!

He invited Annas, Caiaphas, the venerable Gamaliel, and myself to join him at the cemetery to examine their graves to verify that they were not there, but risen.

We all agreed to his invitation and when the graves were found uncovered and empty, Caiaphas adjourned the meeting so that we five could travel to Arimathea with the hope that the two men might be willing to talk to us.

"...they will not be convinced even if someone rises from the dead."

(Luke 16:31;)

CHAPTER 34

Chagrin

JUST AS JOSEPH had said, the two men were found in their house secluded from the general public.

When they saw Joseph approaching with the four of us, all of whom they knew, they wept for joy at our presence, and at the invitation of Caiaphas, agreed to accompany us back to Jerusalem, where they could tell of their adventure and answer our questions.

Upon our return, a remote synagogue within the city was chosen, as public exposure at the temple amid its extensive repairs would defeat the purpose of our enquiry.

The whole Sanhedrin now present, Caiaphas brought out the sacred book of the law, and asked the two men to swear upon it that the account they would give would be true and faithful.

They explained to us that Jesus had visited them in the very bowels of Hell in his glorious resurrected state. He had come to liberate them from the jaws of death and raise them to bodily life.

Jesus then instructed them not to reveal to anyone that he had appeared to them.

Then they withdrew themselves in prayer, although still within our presence, seeking some divine guidance for permission to speak.

In front of us all they both raised their finger to their tongue and made the sign of the cross, signifying their new-sworn allegiance, explaining that they would write out the account of their experience rather than speak it.

Pen and parchment were supplied and they began to write.

I digress, in recognition of the understandable confusion and even doubt held by some in your day and age as to the existence of such a place as Hell.

You see, given the hope of eternal life in the presence of Jesus, believers in Christ look forward to the immediate translation of their soul into his presence in Heaven.

But, in my day, prior to Jesus' resurrection, there was no difficulty in our acceptance of the place called Hell.

We Pharisees believed in a resurrection of the body at some point after death. For Karinus and Leucius to speak of such was no difficulty for us.

Intriguing for us was their meeting with Adam, the father of all mankind, Isaiah the great messianic prophet, as well as the numerous other prophets of Old Testament times.

Isaiah personally assured them that this man Jesus, now standing before them, was the same that he had written about in his great prophecy bearing his name.

Of chief interest to them, and us, was their meeting with Simeon, the very one who had held Jesus in his arms and blessed him.

Simeon assured them that an angel had told him he would not taste of death until he had seen the Messiah upon this earth.

He had held him as a babe in his arms and blessed him to the divine destiny that awaited him.

He told them of the heartbreak with which he revealed to Jesus' mother Mary, that she would endure unimaginable sorrow on account of her son. He described it to be as though a sword had pierced her heart. She no doubt had understood what Simeon had meant, as she stood at the foot of his cross.

To our surprise they wrote about their meeting with John the Baptist, who had been executed by the very King Herod, who had so ridiculed Jesus.

John told them how he had baptized Jesus in the river Jordan. He acknowledged that without doubt he had baptized the Jewish Messiah.

I have already mentioned the accompanying signs that John wrote about in his gospel.

They continued to write of the liberation from Hell and the translation into Heaven of all human beings who had died from the time of Adam until the resurrection of Jesus, provided that they would bow the knee before Jesus.

Satan was berated by Death himself for having engineered the death of Christ, bringing him into Hell before them all, thus sealing their ultimate defeat.

Whereupon these two witnesses, and numerous others resurrected from the graveyard, were commissioned to appear to many persons within the city, bearing similar testimony as they had just given us.

It was at the conclusion of the writing of their testimony, and our worship with them, that they were suddenly taken from our midst, undoubtedly into Paradise, to join the rest.

It was with particular interest and satisfaction that they had also confirmed that the repentant thief, who had hung on the cross next to Jesus, was among the number who entered Paradise that day!

We are not to know the hearts of Annas and Caiaphas, or any of the other members of the Sanhedrin in attendance, when they were read the pages of the testimony of the two men.

Indeed, it is so with all persons who confront soul issues, that judgment of their fellow men becomes hypocritical in light of their own struggles with sin.

As for me, I soon came to realize that so great a salvation was impossible to keep quiet once the soul felt itself liberated from the bondage of sin.

I was saddened to find out, in the immediate days that followed, that Caiaphas and many in the Sanhedrin were not persuaded by the testimony, even of those who had been raised from the dead, confirming the words of Jesus he had once prophesied. Instead, they became the avowed enemies of "The Way," the title given to the new band of followers, who chose to believe in Jesus of Nazareth as our promised Messiah.

As for Joseph and I, another liberation day had been given to us!

We would never more be accosted by Caiaphas!

We were free men!

But we both knew that we would never again sit as members of the Sanhedrin!

Although we had been on the most friendly of terms throughout those earlier days, our associations did not extend beyond our official responsibilities.

Now, there came upon us a deep sense of comradeship, bonding us together as two pilgrims on a new and living way that would surely lead us to an ever-growing faith in Jesus.

I, Nicodemus, who had talked with him face to face in the garden of Gethsemane as he presented himself as the sacrificial lamb. Joseph, who had seen him face to face in his resurrection glory!

A warm twirling wind spun us out of our reverie as we left the synagogue. It was time to go to Pilate!

"…blessed are those who have not seen and yet have believed."

CHAPTER 35

A New Course

THE PURPOSE OF our visit to Pilate was to warn him of the deception Caiaphas had created by his bribery of the soldiers, who had guarded Jesus' tomb, and to tell him of the strange but marvelous things that had taken place since the third day of Jesus' entombment.

We found him to be completely bedraggled in appearance, and profoundly bereft of the usual airs that normally adorned his illustrious position.

It was obvious that he had joined his wife in the suffering of many things because of his judgment of Jesus.

He received us kindly even though I am sure he wished never to see another religious Jew again.

We assured him that we both understood his conundrum in the adjudicating of such a difficult case, given his prime responsibility of assuring the peace over his jurisdiction.

We told him of the events of the past week, and assured him that Joseph had personally encountered the risen Christ, as had many others by now, and that any account from his soldiers to the contrary was the result of bribery on the part of Caiaphas.

"In fact," added Joseph, "his bribing of his own temple guard over my escape from the shack where I was held prisoner is common knowledge." He then told Pilate the facts of his own divine deliverance from the hand of Caiaphas.

Pilate informed us that Caiaphas had asked for a meeting with him following the impending Sabbath.

He told us that already his guards had reported to him and confessed the supernatural events at the tomb that had caused their swoon.

He explained that the guards were often offered bribes, and feared more the penalty of death for such a misdemeanor than to pocket the money. They had offered it to Pilate, who because of their honesty, allowed them to keep it and return to their duty, knowing full well that they could not possibly keep the truth of the event quiet, thus thwarting the High Priest's intentions.

He told us he believed the guards completely, and that our account of events had confirmed his inclinations.

Pilate, like us, was certain that Caiaphas would deny that he and the Sanhedrin had done any such thing.

We warned Pilate that Caiaphas would likely present him with the record of the ancient writings and traditions he thought would justify his rejection of Jesus' resurrection. This despite the witness of those who by now would have discovered with joy the reality of the hope of Israel.

Pilate informed us that he would insist on meeting them in the temple behind closed doors, and would demand that our sacred Torah be presented before him, and that the testimony Caiaphas would give would be written word-for-word into the adjudication of Jesus' trial.

He would then send the entire transcript to Caesar, with a cover letter requesting that he be transferred or be honorably retired.

He made no attempt to hide from Joseph and I his utter disgust with every attempt he had made to govern fairly such a deceptive people.

He gave us to understand that he did not "tar and feather" the whole Jewish population, but confessed his utter disillusionment with a religion that repeatedly presented itself as totally self-serving by its utter disregard for the common people it pretended to lead.

Joseph and I assured him of our confidence in our discovery of the true Messiah of Israel, and assured him of our prayers.

We parted on amicable terms, three victims of such consummate hatred, that it sullied any pretense to power that Caiaphas might claim.

What now? "To whom else can we go?" That question comprised another problem!

Who it was we sought, we knew! But we did not know how!

Jesus had certainly risen from the dead! Of that fact there was no dispute among us.

I personally was dependent upon the faithful witness of those who had seen him alive after his crucifixion, because as yet I had not encountered him.

I am not to be pitied!

Countless others, who would come to believe, would revel in Jesus' comment to Thomas at the hour of his indecision. "Because you have seen me, you have believed; blessed are those who have not seen and yet have believed."

The focus of his followers was now upon his impending ascension into Heaven, that at this point had not yet happened.

We knew he was ensconced with his disciples, for a final briefing, at a place known only to them – and as grace had it, to me also!

I knew where it would be because I had been there!

True, the general area of Bethany was rumored, but its proximity to the Mount of Olives suggested to my mind that the same secret path to Gethsemane would once again be used.

What more appropriate place could there be for a final earthly parting than that blessed rock upon which Jesus had poured out his tears and his very soul! Only this time all of the eleven remaining disciples would witness the place where he received from his Heavenly Father God, the power, the grace, and love that so marked his ministry.

It was of course apparent to Joseph, and to myself, that despite our latter beneficence to Jesus in the treatment of his body, we could not share in such a sacred moment.

They would later tell us of all that happened.

If we truly believed that he was indeed our long-awaited Messiah (and from our participation at his trial and afterward it might easily be construed that we did indeed believe), both Joseph and I knew that such a commitment constrained us far beyond any emotional, physical or verbal assent.

Given the continued rage of Caiaphas and the Sanhedrin, and their determination to cling to power, our very lives would remain on the line.

We were all too conscious of the price we might have to pay for any such allegiance to Jesus. And although at this point perhaps somewhat vague, we were beginning to understand that our commitment could not be measured in human terms, but rather the very eternal destiny of our soul awaited our decision.

This was the issue for the disciples now gathered with their Lord and Master.

In those moments with Jesus, the price of their allegiance would truly be made apparent.

There will always be opposition to faith!

No matter where or when a human soul encounters Jesus, self will be laid on the altar, or any lesser sacrifice will be denied.

I remind you, Joseph and I had left the Temple and the Sanhedrin just hours before, knowing full well we could never return. We had just moments ago left Pilate and the pitiful claims of the authority of Rome to rule the human conscience.

To whom else could we go?

Well, for the moment at least, there was but one option open to us. We each departed for our own house.

Strange! There it was again! That wind that still persisted following the mighty storm and earthquake that crucifixion day!

"...But I am among you as one who serves."

(Luke 22:27;)

CHAPTER 36

Commitment

THERE ARE TIMES when life seems to stand still. A valley of decision! A moment of transition! The beginning of a new adventure! Decision time!

"That's it" I mused, as I entered the door to my home. "Nothing is ever going to be the same again!"

I scarce had my hand on the handle when it swung swiftly open, as though self-propelled.

Actually it had already been set ajar by my wife who was anxiously awaiting my return. She always knew the slightest sound of my approaching footsteps.

She flung herself into my arms, and without a single word we embraced, transfixed in the emotion of this moment we both knew was ushering in the greatest life-change we had ever experienced.

Need I make any comment? Did it require any explanation? Was there any need for detailed discussion?

We both knew the Holy Spirit had now enveloped the two of us. We both knew that he was bringing to us a depth of spiritual perception never before experienced.

There was a sense of soul cleansing, despite the guilt, shame and trauma of which we had been a part.

Unashamedly we shed many tears as we stood there; copious, hot, soul cleansing tears.

To some there will be instant empathy and understanding for what I have so inadequately described.

To others it may present a conundrum. For that reason I present some further detail.

The social, financial and religious implications of our decision I have earlier explained.

It is with the spiritual implications of our impending decision that I hope to enlighten you.

Oh yes! Be assured that in our case, though entwined with religious overtones, the details I now share of this new spiritual journey rest within the most private and intimate relationship of one's soul in concourse with his/her creator.

We were not about to throw away every vestige of our religious past. After all, we were entering the fulfillment of all that the prophets had portrayed in our holy scriptures that we loved dearly.

The point to be made here is that life always leads us to the portal of the unknown, and a step forward demands an assessment of what acquisitions of mind and spirit we are to take into the new experience, and what to discard in its achievement.

There was no doubt that life had been extraordinarily kind to us. It was apparent that the accumulation of our wealth, social standing and religious prowess, was more often the gift of circumstance rather than decisions made.

We had also lived long enough to know the fickle torment of gain and loss affected by political, economic, social, and yes, even religious overtones, and quite often beyond one's control.

All such experiences greatly impact personal choice!

Now, as we stood in the doorway enveloped by our embrace, we were conscious that to follow Jesus as the promised Messiah and Savior of our soul meant that personal choice would become subject to the leadings of the Holy Spirit. From this moment on, every decision we made would be dictated by our relationship with the Son of God.

During his earthly life, he had made it quite clear concerning riches, that it was easier to push a camel through the night gate at the city wall, than for a rich man to enter the Kingdom of Heaven.

Only one individual at a time could gain entrance, even then in a humped position.

Neither was there place for inordinate ambition!

He had taught that if you wanted to be first in his kingdom you remained in the place of a servant. The achievement of any and all kingdom advancement was couched in servitude and humility.

He also taught that one's love for God must supersede their love for family!

No, I hasten to assure you that such a demand was in no wise meant to replace such filial affection. To the contrary, such spiritual relationship with God could only enhance one's family relationships, depending on the attitude of family members toward one's commitment.

Any opposition to one's commitment to Christ was to be countered by a Christian's god-given love for their opposing family member/s.

Only by absolute obedience to the requirements dictated by God's Holy Spirit was such divinely inspired love to be achieved.

There was yet another hurdle confronting us!

I write about the religious affiliations that so greatly influence decisions of the soul.

Although you might expect your religion to facilitate the advancement of your spirituality, the opposite all too often is the case!

You will already understand this, given the above record of events that had drawn us to this moment of decision.

That religion is the chosen guardian of spirituality is apparent!

Jesus frequently made reference to "My Church" in defining the continuing work of his disciples.

Unfortunately we all too often "put the cart before the horse" as the old adage has it.

Before the advent of any religious system on earth, of whatever stripe, there was a beautiful experience of personal relationship between the Creator and the created.

Upon the decimation of that relationship through the disobedience of our first parents, Adam and Eve, there arose a supposedly remedial hierarchy of religious tradition designed to bring men back to God.

That system was entrusted to us Jews and developed by Moses under God's personal tutorage, with Abraham, the father of our nation, as patriarch of what became to be known as "God's chosen people."

That exclusive heritage drove a wedge between us Jews, offspring of Jacob, and the Arabs, offspring of Esau, both the sons of Abraham.

Add to that the myriad of religions developed among other nations descending from Adam, and it is easily seen how our world became filled with every religious expression the human imagination is capable of.

All this was because relationship with The Creator of mankind had given way to the self-serving manipulation of religious adherents, especially those who had obtained power.

Now, finally, there had stood in our midst the "Melchizedek" of our time, the very "priest of God Most High" to whom Abraham himself had presented his tithes!

Once again he was calling God's human creation into loving relationship with their maker. His name was Jesus Christ of Nazareth! Our Messiah! The Savior of the world!

This was the original purpose for which he had created our priesthood in the first place!

He had lived among us in resplendent demonstration of a loving benevolent use of supernatural power!

He required nothing of his followers other than their acknowledgment of the supremacy of a loving God and himself as his divinely chosen son!

He offered himself up to his executioners as the propitiation for our sins!

Now, through that sacrifice, I was being challenged to enter into a personal relationship with God by means of simple faith and trust in Jesus, as my Savior and Lord, religious refinement notwithstanding!

Did he require of me the abandonment of my religious faith? No!

But now my religion was demanding my allegiance at the cost of my hope in him, who I now believed to be the savior of my soul.

Yes, as I have earlier said, you might well remind me that my nation sat under Roman bondage because of that same rebellion to the will of God that had repeatedly cast us into senseless idolatry and subsequent servitude to those whose idols we had adopted.

Yes, I have also told you of the faithfulness of God when we responded to his faithful prophets who time and again called us back to faith.

But now the final moment had come! It was a last chance decision time!

Only Jesus held out hope for our nation as for one final time we were about to suffer the longest disbursement of our history by reason of our rejection of our Messiah.

With tears in his eyes, he had cried "O Jerusalem, Jerusalem, how oft would I have gathered you as a hen gathers her chick under her wings, but ye would not."

He then began his triumphal entry into Jerusalem that led to his sacrifice.

Of course it must come as no surprise to you that excommunication from the religion that had been my very life would come with copious tears.

That time had come!

My wife and I were determined to walk into the unknown!

Still in our embrace, I closed the front door, conscious that each was loved as never before.

Our souls lay bare before God. Kneeling on the floor we confessed our faith in Jesus as Messiah, the Lord and Savior of our souls, the Son of God, So help us!

*"He who is not with me is
against me,..."*

(Matthew 12:30;)

CHAPTER 37

What's Next

WHAT NOW? WHAT do we do? Where do we go?

The door to our lifetime religion was now closed to us!

Was there any fellowship among Christ's followers open to us, since we were once counted among the enemy?

Was there any place left for us among our society and friends?

What of our children? Would we be cast off from these precious ones we had instructed so diligently in Jewish Law?

We knew that to address these questions at this early stage would be self-defeating.

Instead, we for the first time prayed to God our Creator in the name of our newfound Savior Jesus Christ, committing these issues to his care. We didn't know what was appropriate in word or in format, but almost instantly there came to us both the words of our scriptures, your Old Testament, "Be still and know that I am God."

No, there was not yet revealed a plan; no sense of his will; no particular instruction, other than to simply quiet our hearts before him in child-like trust, and await his leading.

No more self-help programs! No more formality and ritual!

If Jesus could declare God the Creator to be his Father, then so could we. If Jesus was his Son, then we were his brother and sister!

Of course we had no presupposed expectations of our future. These would come only from further experience and commitment. The ignorance of our new beginnings did not nullify the truth and sincerity of our faith. By the simple child-like faith Jesus had demanded of his disciples we put our hand into his, and peace of heart and mind came to us.

Then came a knock at the door!

Was the price of our decision already awaiting us on the other side of the lintel? Was our faith to be soundly tested already? Should we open the door at all?

With our fear readily admitted I tell you, we opened the door!

And there he stood! John! Again!

He was quickly admitted, and welcomed, and hugged oh so tight that I am certain he sensed that a miracle of grace stood before him.

His errand was urgent in nature!

He had assembled with the others at Bethany, the details of which were to be shared with us in due course.

There, in company with the other ten disciples, and numerous others to whom Jesus had earlier appeared, they had witnessed the ascension of Jesus into Heaven.

They heard him promise that he would return to this earth in like manner as they beheld him ascending. Only then, he would descend upon the clouds in great glory with his host of mighty angels accompanying him, to take up his throne in Jerusalem, where he would hold a court of judgment over all peoples of the earth.

He had given his disciples explicit instructions to remain in Jerusalem until they had been "endued with power from on high."

They had chosen to return to the very room they had used for their last Passover meal with Jesus.

The owner was a believer in Jesus and intuitively knew that he should hold it for the further use of the disciples.

John had come at the behest of Peter and the others to invite my wife and I to join them. Joseph was already there with a number of other believers.

The route to the location was totally unfamiliar to me, being in one of the less frequented parts of the city. In fact John had asked that we dress less pretentiously for our walk, so as to avoid attracting others to us. They seldom saw persons of such importance in this less pretentious part of Jerusalem. For the same reasons this meeting was being convened in the very early dawn.

In our subsequent frequent visits to the area, with John's help, we actually used varied routes to our destination. This was to confuse the agents of the High Priest who were by now intent upon the next step in their plan to put a stop to the work of the disciples and stamping out all vestige of "The Way," a new "buzz word," as you call it, that would become the identity of this new, "subversive," movement within the Jewish religion.

Despite the sanctuary of that upper room, the surrounding danger enticed the disciples to place a guard at the door whenever it was in use.

I shall never forget that first entry into the company of the disciples.

I had expected that beyond the presence of my wife and I and Joseph, the group might include Jesus' mother and the women who had attended the needs of his entourage during his ministry. But the composition and size of the group was as much a surprise to us as we were to them.

We encountered all the siblings of Jesus with Mary their mother.

We recognized the Roman Centurion who had been in charge of the execution squad. He had declared Jesus to be the

Son of God, there at the cross. On this occasion he was dressed in regular street clothes. He had brought with him some of the other soldiers that had guarded the tomb, and even one from Joseph's imprisonment, all of them incognito.

Also present were a number of people whom Jesus had healed bodily, and from whom he had cast out demons. Of particular note was Mary Magdalene who out of utmost gratitude had anointed Jesus for his burial with very expensive oil, now fully cognizant of the significance of her action.

Surprisingly there were present some of the former disciples who, strangely, had forsaken his ministry when disillusioned with some of his claims and teachings, despite the fact that they had shared the divine powers Jesus had anointed them with for that first missions trip.

As might be expected, there were some of those who had been resurrected from their graves on the eve of his execution, accompanied by joyful relatives.

I also recognized the presence of some of the temple priests, although now they no longer wore their priestly vestments. They had obviously secretly sided with Jesus during his teaching at the temple.

In all, there were present about one hundred and twenty souls.

The purpose of the assembly was in compliance with Jesus' implicit instructions, given to the disciples immediately prior to his ascension.

He told them they were to remain in Jerusalem until they had been "endued with power from on high," as Doctor Luke puts it in his Gospel.

The disciples knew something of Jesus' intent, having been taught that, after he was taken from them into Heaven, he would ask the Heavenly Father to send the Holy Spirit to them, to comfort and instruct them for future ministry.

Jesus had not been more explicit about this, "power," other than to say that such a baptism would be over and beyond the water baptism John the Baptist had required of his repentant listeners, a carry over of the Jewish practice of admitting committed gentiles into the Jewish religion.

Even then his disciples had displayed what to Jesus must have been a discouraging attitude. They questioned if by this means, Jesus intended to bring political liberation and restoration to the nation of Israel.

The motive behind such a question was really their concern for some elevation to positions of importance in his scheme of things. (Shades of James and John and their mother all over again).

Jesus had simply ignored the implications of their question by telling them not to involve themselves in issues that were the sole concern of Almighty God himself.

He hastened to assure them that the baptism of which he spoke would enable them to fearlessly witness to his resurrection and divine authority as the Son of God in Jerusalem, Samaria, and to the uttermost corners of the earth.

As we were soon to find out, this sizable band of believers was in no way ready to receive such a visitation from the Almighty!

In fact, as I reflect upon those hours, days, then weeks, consuming more than a month, how could there have been found any justification for a baptism of any kind whatever, but for the quiet work of the Spirit of Christ within the individual soul of each one present?

Something had to happen! And quickly! And wouldn't you know, as some might have guessed, it all started with Peter!

Now if that leaves the reader's mouth agape, your surprise is no more than was mine!

Mind you! His taking charge brought no protests from the other disciples, or any others in the room.

And I can assure you this was not the old Peter that stood before us!

As he drew the crowd to his attention, his voice and demeanor held no evidence of his former bravado. There was no brashness, none of the old ego we might have expected of him.

This was a new Peter!

He was prompt to acknowledge the illegitimacy of any claim to leadership. In fact he said it was only by the prior insistence of his fellow disciples that he stood before us.

He assumed that his colossal denial of Jesus at his trial before Pilate was now common knowledge. He told of the reconciliation between himself and Jesus that had occurred on the shore of the Sea of Galilee.

Jesus had once again called all the disciples to ministry, by a repeat of yet another stupendous catch of fish, such as had occurred at their initial calling.

With great humility and considerable emotion, he told how Jesus had demanded his renewal of allegiance three times in succession, in consequence of his earlier three-time denial of his master.

He did not clarify whether or not the other disciples had witnessed his renewed commission.

He confessed that he stood before us only by the grace of God, a mellowed, repentant, humbled servant of Jesus.

He begged the forgiveness of us all for whatever pain his cowardly act may have inflicted upon us.

He told us that no particular format for our gathering had been assigned. He thought that our assembly should be open to whatever spoken word or act of worship each one present might share with the others.

He did suggest that we should be much in prayer, privately and corporately, for the duration of our vigil.

It was agreed upon, that we would assemble each morning at this same time and disperse at nightfall, or otherwise as surreptitiously as possible, and by no means in more than groups of twos or threes.

Utmost to our continued welfare was the secrecy of our assembly.

Without fanfare, he did acknowledge the presence of Joseph, and my wife and I. He profoundly thanked us for our part in the defense at the trial, and the burial of our Lord.

He then turned to the Roman Centurion and the group of soldiers with him.

He assured them he bore no malice toward them. Their participation in the despicable execution of his Lord was only by the orders of their superiors.

Given his triple denial of Jesus, and the desertion of all the disciples at his arrest, there was no room for finger pointing.

Besides, the greater guilt was upon those who had precipitated the crime in the first place, and they certainly were not to be found in this room!

He said he now understood, if more by the heart than by reason, that Jesus did indeed take to the cross the sins of all mankind.

Peter insisted that first on the list were his own.

With heartfelt thanks to God, he acknowledged our brave commitment to the Savior, despite facing possible execution, given the vehement hatred toward Jesus by the High Priest Caiaphas.

He also acknowledged the presence of the temple priests assembled and assured those present that John had vouched for their sincerity of conviction concerning the Lordship of Jesus.

I confess that I personally had some concerns that some of them might be spies infiltrating this secret hideaway! But this was soon dissipated when they proved to be most useful to us in the searching of the scriptures pertaining to the prophecies written about Jesus, a great help in affirming our newborn faith.

Peter was quick to assure us that any further admissions of anyone else, from whatever background, would be subject to a thorough screening.

Joseph and I privately discussed with Peter, James and John the financial arrangements for the use of the room in which we were assembled, and we suggested that, further to our commitment to the covering of costs for same, we would be happy to arrange for light refreshments throughout each day. The disciples were quick to accept our offer with much gratitude.

Actually, the real test of our liberality was yet to come as growing numbers of the church would experience dismissal from their places of work; foreclosure on loans; and in some instances confiscation of their homes and personal property at the hands of "loyal" Jews, used as pawns in the vendetta inflicted upon us by Caiaphas and the Sanhedrin.

But there is yet much more to be told about this assembly!

"Forgive us our debts, as we also have forgiven our debtors."

(Matthew 6:12;)

CHAPTER 38

Reconciliation

I SUPPOSE BY MEANS of a private meeting of the eleven disciples, it was decided that there should be selected, from among those present, a replacement for Judas, the disciple who had betrayed Jesus.

Now I surmise that you would be as surprised as I was that this decision was made, given the very nature of our assembly.

Aught we not to be waiting for the anointing of the Holy Spirit Jesus had promised before making such a decision?

But I was quick to recall that all of us were there at the invitation of the disciples. Consequently, any criticism of such an important matter would be inappropriate.

It was undoubtedly the priests who shared with the disciples much of the prophecies concerning the Messiah, and pointed out the particular prophecy that concerned the betrayal of Judas, confirming that the now vacated position must be filled by another.

The reasons for this requirement, apart from the prophetic instructions themselves, would not be fully known for many years yet to come.

The Apostle John, the selfsame disciple with us that day, would, in his old age, receive an apocalyptic vision from Jesus.

It is contained in the New Testament in the book of "Revelation."

It depicts the inner circle around the great white throne of heaven, on which Jesus would sit, surrounded by the twelve patriarchs of the twelve tribes of Israel, and the *twelve* Apostles of the Christian Church.

Obviously, Judas was to be replaced, bringing to strength the "twelve" Apostles surrounding the great white throne.

No specific instructions from Jesus about making the selection had been given. So the disciples proceeded with the familiar Jewish custom used to appoint someone to religious office.

In this case, they confined their selection to those who had participated in Jesus' ministry from the beginning. Narrowing the selection down to two, Barsabbas/Justus and Matthias, they prayed to the Lord Jesus that he would show which of the two he had chosen.

They then placed in a jar a small stone for each and every candidate selected, (in this case two), and drew one only, that bore the mark or color allotted to that particular candidate. That candidate would be concluded to be the one chosen by God.

It now became clear to me why some of those who had forsaken the ministry in its early days of opposition had been admitted to our group: God in his infinite wisdom and mercy had brought to our attention another recipient of his forgiveness and restoration to the faith.

Since there were no other disciples left of Jesus' followers except for the twelve after the defection of the seventy, and given that no disciple now present in that room had not forsaken Jesus, there could be no possible objection to the recall of Matthias.

For all the activity of this assembly to this point, there remained the resolve of a most critical issue, the reconciliation of the disciples with Mary, the mother of Jesus, and her family.

Most apparent was the need for resolve of the unspeakable hurt they had caused Mary.

Much chagrin remained between the disciples and Jesus' brothers.

True, there were no disciples present at the crucifixion except John, but neither were any of her sons present to support their mother.

Oh what cost pride and self-centeredness exacts upon the human condition!

The disciples had all forsaken him at his arrest out of fear of capture and punishment.

Jesus had only been an embarrassment and frustration to his family, despite the fact that Mary had undoubtedly shared with them the experience of her immaculate conception.

Notwithstanding, Jewish men stood in absolute authority over women in all issues of life. It was undoubtedly out of pride and ignorance that they had opposed their brother's ministry especially in light of the opposition of our religious hierarchy.

Did they not drag Mary along to one of the sites of Jesus' preaching and healing to insist he return home and forget all this nonsense that was causing them such embarrassment? I have reported earlier his affront to this situation.

This was not the time for finger pointing!

Mary was their first priority!

We all wept to see the quiet inconspicuous approach of each disciple to her side, their copious tears flowing, and without audible words, embracing this woman chosen of God to bear their savior.

Each received the comforting embrace and pat-on-the-back that signaled plenteous forgiveness.

Through tears welling up from a heart still pierced with the sword of sacrifice, she addressed us all, confessing her own son to be The Son of God and her personal Savior and Lord. She then extended to all present her sincere forgiveness emanating from her own confession of faith.

Then James, her eldest son, stood before us and begged our forgiveness that he the closest sibling to Jesus should have ever denied him to the very point of his undisputed resurrection.

There followed his brothers Joseph, Simon and Judas, each of them confirming their new faith in Jesus as their Savior.

Oh the tears! Oh the hugs and consolation! Oh the unspeakable joy that settled over that room as each of us embraced one another, bringing such a peace and solidarity to our newfound relationships. This was truly a precursor to the unity of a newfound church under the dominion of our Servant-Lord.

The healing of relationships soon gave way to wave upon wave of testimony.

True, the disciples had been witnesses to the physical and emotional healing of several gathered in that room. Still, there were more than a few of us whose relationship to Jesus was to them unknown.

In fact, such witness was essential to our true identity as Christians, and without it the justification of our presence in so sacred a place would have been suspect.

There was no sense of judgment or suspicion toward us. The room was just too full of love and friendship for that. In fact such a positive attitude toward us confirmed to me that our presence was more due to divine intervention, rather than by human agreement alone. We had only to reach back, most of us the distance of weeks, to marvel at the grace of God that had brought us here in the first place.

It was indeed a joy, and deeply therapeutic to the soul, to hear the testimonies that followed.

I begin with those who had been physically healed by Jesus!

It was thrilling to hear how Jesus healed them, liberating them from earlier days when they were so bound and debilitated by their illness. But even more thrilling was their willingness to explain the spiritual implications of that healing.

A new love for God had been implanted in their hearts. No longer was Jesus just an uncommonly gifted itinerant preacher. God their creator had visited them in the flesh of the Nazarene! The long-awaited Messiah had come at last! The credibility of their religious belief was confirmed! It was not only the healing of their body that had taken place. Common to all who testified, their very souls had been reborn, by an overwhelming sense of the love of God.

Of special significance was the witness of those who had been possessed by demons.

Their testimony gave credence to the reality of Satan and his demon angels. I assure you, despite the thrill of their stories, their personal accounts were not easy to listen to.

There was a common thread throughout their combined witness.

They had ignored the ample and explicit teachings of the scriptures and the warnings of their religious teachers, and had delved into the world of the occult. Once there, they had found no escape and their fully rational minds were drained of all human processing until they were completely controlled by their demon/s who through their captives gained further access to other unsuspecting souls.

Blessedly, their tale turned to the grace and power of almighty God in Jesus Christ; how their horror had turned to total ecstasy of spirit, mind and body. Jesus had made all the difference. He alone could deliver them from the bonds of satanic influence.

Soul gripping was the testimony of those who had been raised from the dead by Jesus!

Oh yes! Lazarus was there amongst us!

He held us breathless, and in some considerable fear, as he spoke of those three days he had spent in the bowels of Hell.

He explained that until the resurrection of Jesus from the dead, there was no repository for the soul save the realm of Death and Hell. Hence, only the all-powerful name of Jesus could order them to give up the dead.

His own resurrection from the dead was a testimony to the divine credentials of our Lord.

It was at that point, those who had recently been released from their graves, gave their testimony.

Jesus had come to them to witness to the grace of God that had been poured out upon all flesh by the shedding of his blood.

He demanded the release of every soul who had been faithful to the testimony of God their creator to their very last breath upon this earth.

Lazarus explained, with their total agreement, that Death and Hell were now conquered, and no soul, whose trust was placed in Jesus Christ, would ever enter there.

He reminded us, "Did not Jesus say to the repentant thief on the cross, 'this day you shall be with me in Paradise'?"

I tell you, there was a loud accolade of "hallelujahs, praises to God, thank you Jesus," amongst us.

Now I want to assure you of the spontaneity of spirit that prevailed in that room. All I have described above had no format or ritualistic precedent.

There were prolonged periods of silence amid much soul-searching. Only when and as the Holy Spirit moved upon each of us did we speak!

We? Yes!

The moment came when Joseph, the priests, and myself, gave testimony of the grace of God that had come upon us, and our consequent belief in Jesus as the Son of God and our personal Savior.

Joseph was quick to tell of my attempt to bring to the Sanhedrin some reminder of the rule of law, demanding that witnesses be allowed to speak in defense of Jesus.

In response, I freely admitted my cowardice at the thought of the price I would pay by offending the High Priest when so many of the Sanhedrin sided with him.

I felt it indiscreet to mention my clandestine defense of Jesus before Pilate, given that my identification with Jesus was so tenuous. The witness of my faith and belief in Jesus was well received, and to my joy, added to, by my wife.

She spoke her own words of personal witness, a precedent graciously allowed women in this circle, but not always permitted by the new church soon to be born.

"...As I have loved you, so you must love one another."

(John 13:34;)

CHAPTER 39

Soul Searching

BY THIS TIME you're anxious that I "get on with it!"

That's because you already know the "fact" of the coming of the Holy Spirit upon those of us in the upper room.

My chief concern is that you should know personally the baptism of power that came with his anointing!

For that I must beg your patience!

I pray that the penning of my own experience will bring understanding and encouragement to the truly seeking heart.

I pray that it will lead you into such fullness of joy, that it will only be surpassed by our eventual admission into the very presence of our Lord Jesus.

I assure you that your conjectures concerning such a blessing are no different than those expressed in that upper room!

The priests among us were well versed in the scriptures and able to trace for us the remarkable messianic prophecies, from Genesis to the birth of Jesus.

They thrilled us with tales of the work of empowerment, endowed to the prophets, judges and kings of Israel, from earliest times throughout our history, until the formidable silence of the four hundred plus years, commonly known as the Period of the Macabees.

They reminded us that it was Jesus who broke the silence!

I shuddered as I remembered what we Jews did about that!

Much conjecture! No conclusions! We were without the knowledge that the present-day church holds in common.

Why then do some tend to make such a blessing exclusive to those who demonstrate supernatural gifts?

I remind you that the baptism of the Holy Spirit first came upon a room of humble born-again souls, in response to their repentance and faith. We had no more to offer!

All that I have told thus far actually accounts for only the first week or so of our tryst.

Ah! Have I not used a word usually associated with the meeting of lovers?

Yes! It is so! It describes the enormous need of reconciliation among all of us in that room, not only with each other (as I have described above) but also of the soul with its maker.

I am happy to advise that at some point during those days of strain, waiting gave way to a most blessed bonding of relationships among us.

We did not realize it at first, but there was much soul searching, confession, forgiveness and reconciliation to be accomplished among all of us before the coming of the divine visitation we anticipated at any moment.

A case in point!

The twelve original disciples had demonstrated inordinate ambition as to future leadership positions in Christ's kingdom, with no little ego expressed in this very room in the last days together with Jesus, prior to his crucifixion.

The disciples told us, with much chagrin, how Jesus had taken the basin and towel and in the spirit of utter servitude had washed the feet of each one of them.

You would think that such a pungent reminder of their pride would have permanently put the matter to rest.

Alas! Once again it raised its head at Bethany in anticipation of what they believed was to be deliverance from Roman rule under the authority of Jesus.

In neither incident did Jesus give any satisfaction to the promotion seekers.

Now, here in this room, ambition had given way to humility and servanthood.

The disciples were observed in huddle a number of times throughout the waiting period. The resolve of numerous issues was evident with hugs, tears, expressions of gratitude and prayer between two or more of them. It came to me as a source of pleasure and confidence that such reconciliation and bonding was increasingly obvious.

I do not confine my remarks to the disciples only!

I observed groups of family members cloistered in prayer in remote corners of the room with similar results.

Yes, we often saw individuals praying privately, resolving whatever issues confronted their own personal convictions, I among them!

The numerous conclaves of priests at prayer and conversation among themselves, was of particular interest to me!

It is to be remembered that they held vital responsibilities at the temple, and now it seemed they were outcasts, cut off from their ancestral rights. Undoubtedly they were seeking some sort of common ground between their birthright and their new relationship with Jesus. Service to God had consumed all of their life if you considered the years of preparation they had endured from their youth.

To their credit, a sense of reconciliation and resolve to serve God and Jesus their redeemer became obvious. Indeed I detected an air of quiet joy in their demeanor.

Of course I do not exclude my wife and myself from the process.

Some of our most precious moments were spent in conversation with Joseph of Arimathea. He had such a depth of devotion to God and our scriptures. He was most pleased to mentor us in the prophecies that comprised the foundation of his conviction that Jesus was indeed the Christ, the long-awaited

Messiah. He shared the trauma of our decision to place our faith in Jesus as our savior.

He brought to us a peace of mind that our decision was indeed the right one, and we sensed he would fully support us in our new journey of faith.

Of particular delight to my wife and myself was a newfound depth of love between us, a legacy of our commitment to Christ.

Given the traditional religious authority of husband over wife and family, a role that would require much refinement under the guidance of the Apostles, we were delighted to have become equals in our pursuit of godliness under the banner of Jesus. Though my role as head of the household would continue, it would not be on the basis of authority, but of responsibility!

We were truly delighted with the times of prayer we experienced together, just the two of us with Jesus.

There was no doubt that we were all in a period of preparation for the promised Holy Spirit!

Another issue to be resolved was worship. It would be at risk to our lives for us to attend the temple or the synagogues.

Despite the trauma that had thrown our religion into complete disarray, we missed the daily worship and instruction in the scriptures.

In the upper room we had the opportunity of united worship, with Jesus at the center of our devotion to God.

The disciples and priests soon organized a daily service, and encouraged us all to attend it, plus other periods of Bible study. It was vital that we learn of the prophecies that would confirm the accuracy of our newfound faith in Jesus as the Messiah.

These daily exercises helped to develop a cohesive spirit of loving support, assuring a consistent daily attendance, at least for a part of each day.

We did not know it then, but we would be sequestered in that upper room for thirty days or more.

As the days multiplied, and anticipation of the promised Spirit heightened, there was an increasing reluctance to leave that hallowed room, despite the fact that Jesus had not said that attendance was compulsory. We simply were not to leave Jerusalem.

I am pleased to tell you that in the moment of time that concluded our waiting, everyone of us who were originally present on that first day of our sojourn, were in the upper room.

I shudder to think what disappointment would have seized the heart of any who should miss the blessing!

There was now one more issue to resolve: the observance of Pentecost!

It was a cause of great sadness that we would not be able to observe in our temple, what was the happiest of Jewish Holidays, the celebration of the harvest of grains, for fear of arrest and probable execution for our stand for Jesus Christ.

It was a festival that marked fifty days, beginning with the barley harvest, when a sheaf of barley was presented on the altar along with other animal sacrifices.

The harvest of each different crop of grain, each in their turn, culminated with the harvest of wheat.

The celebration was often referred to as "The Festival of Weeks."

It seemed to us that we could observe the celebration amongst ourselves, since we had priests in our group who were thoroughly familiar with the procedure. However, we would have to exercise the greatest caution in bringing small portions of the various grains to our location, so as not to arouse suspicion as to our whereabouts.

It was during our discussions, that we were greatly encouraged by a significant assimilation of our newfound faith with our beloved ancient custom!

You see the festival of Pentecost actually starts at Passover, the celebration of our liberty from Egyptian slavery, when on the eve preceding our exodus we sacrificed a lamb per household, the blood from which we applied to the lintel and doorposts of our houses.

When the Angel of death came to destroy all firstborn of human and animal kind throughout Egypt, observing the blood of the slain lamb, he passed over those homes. We were literally saved by the shedding of the blood of the lamb.

You will recall from my account that our Lord Jesus was slain on the day before Passover. But you will also note that darkness had fallen across the land some three hours earlier than the commencement of our scheduled Passover, rendering the sacrifice void.

Jesus had become the lamb of sacrifice whose blood now cleansed every believer!

You can only imagine the joy and praise with which we prepared to celebrate the new Pentecost!

"But you will receive power when the Holy Spirit comes on you;…"

(Acts 1:8;)

CHAPTER 40

Pentecost

OUR PENTECOST HAD begun with Jesus! Never again would the celebration of this highpoint in Jewish tradition ever be the same for us as in former times!

We no longer needed to bring our sacrificial lamb to the temple altar! Jesus, the true sacrifice for our sins had paid the debt of our transgressions, once for all, on the altar of divine love and grace – a cross!

Those of us in that upper room were the very first Christians on the face of the earth!

We were, so to speak, in uncharted waters, with neither compass nor sexton. We had no map! We had no directions! We had no earthly leader!

It is little wonder we were told by Jesus to wait in Jerusalem until we had been endowed with the power of the Holy Ghost!

To this point all any of us knew was the religious experience, and it was all too clear that religion had failed us. Instead of liberating our spirit, it had enslaved it.

Jesus had set us free!

Yet even the daily activity of our present retreat bore many markings of our religious past.

Until now!

The Spirit of God had indeed been active among us, bringing open confession, repentance, reconciliation and spiritual resolve. He had bonded us together in a spirit of love that created a unity of spirit we had never known in our former religious pursuits.

It is little wonder then that our daily worship and Bible studies gave increasing precedent to prayer! This produced a deep soul-searching within each individual heart!

So deep and personal were those private hours of prayer that I can only give account of myself, respecting as I do, the confidences of those who chose to share with me.

Even though my wife and I had joint devotions together daily, we each realized that our personal prayer time was to be held sacrosanct unless one chose to share with the other.

This new form of prayer felt strange at first. It was more a conversation than the formal prayers I had been used to giving. I had mostly used the Psalms from our scriptures to express myself to God, a practice I did not abandon, and heartily recommend to you. However, in this uncharted territory my needs seemed to go beyond the point of formality. As the expression has it, I just had to "wing it," and in so doing I fell heir to a deepening fellowship with God I had never experienced before.

It became a two-way conversation between God and I.

No! He did not speak audibly to me, but within the deep recesses of my soul I knew God was there and I was free to proverbially "dump my whole load" on him.

I found myself seriously counting the cost of the decisions I had made over the course of the past weeks since the crucifixion of Jesus!

There still loomed large the burden of possessions, politics and religion that I had seemingly abandoned, but never as yet surrendered to Jesus.

In my heart there were issues of relationships within the family and among friends and colleagues that might become irreconcilable, given my decision for Christ.

I knew that these had to be entrusted to Jesus!

There were sin issues, some of which had become ingrained by habitual abandonment of personal and religious principles.

There were personal ambitions that I had long held as my right of passage in pursuit of success, notwithstanding the cost to others.

My chief need of resolve was to remove my impersonal aloofness from God, and in effect from Jesus Christ. I might profess my faith in him as Savior, but I must make him supreme Lord of my life, or I could by no means experience the fullness of his Holy Spirit. Nor could I become a true follower of Christ.

If there was any battle of the soul over these issues, it was on my part. I sensed only a loving persistence of the Spirit throughout my prayer time. The very hunger of my soul for his righteousness precluded victory!

I surmised similar struggles among the group, and it was a true joy to see the evidence of victory in their smiling faces and damp eyes, including mine!

The reverie of these precious days was suddenly interrupted when our sentinel at the door informed Peter that there appeared to be persons spying on our entry and departure to and from the building.

Was one among us an informer? Had our numbers been infiltrated by the enemy? What of the owner? Was he a true believer in Jesus? Was this nucleus of the church of Christ to be snuffed out before it even had a beginning?

Peter first conferred with the owner, and satisfied himself that he was indeed a sympathizer and had taken every precaution to protect us. He then conferred with the Roman Centurion who told him that there had been no recent orders issued to the Praetorian Guards to hunt us down, and his informant from the Temple guards assured him Caiaphas had not yet activated them in any search for us, although we would in the future fall victim to his cunning.

It was concluded by Peter and the other disciples that our movements may have aroused the curiosity of the neighborhood, but given that our meeting room was on the upper floor of the building, the main floor gave all the appearances of "business as usual."

Despite what seems to be a rude intrusion into the middle of my account of spiritual matters, I choose to illustrate the strategy of the enemy of our soul.

Spiritual seeking and resolve will always meet with the interruptions of daily routine, and often with "emergencies" that seem to take precedent over our devotional life.

To this point our safety and welfare was due in large part to our early rising, well before the dawn, to assure the uninterrupted blessing of our spiritual pursuits.

Believe me I have found that when our daily appointment with God takes precedence, the routine of daily life is sanctified by the anointing of the Holy Spirit.

Peter reminded us that we were under orders from Jesus to *wait* for the empowerment of the Holy Spirit. We were to continue in worship, study and prayer for as long as it took, despite what sometimes seemed to be an inordinate delay!

Long after the conclusion of these days I was to learn the value of the discipline of the seeking heart, as I repeatedly sought the will and power of God in the many issues that were beyond human resolve.

As the days of life itself eventually draw to a close, so also these days in the upper room were soon to come to an end, but with a climax that was beyond our wildest possible imagination!

CHAPTER 41

The Wind

WE WERE ALL present in the upper room when it happened!

It can only be described as the unified prompting of the Holy Spirit!

Usually, each of us had gathered there at various times and durations of the day over the weeks that had passed.

Today *he* had brought everyone, without exception, to the meeting place all at the same time!

Furthermore, there was no attempt by anyone assembled, to assume leadership or participation in any of the activities to which we had become accustomed.

There was a solemn stillness in the room that emitted a sweet sense of mutual love among us.

A great sense of anticipation prevailed!

We've all spoken the cliché, "the silence was deafening!" Well it was!

But those days together had hungered our souls for God to such a point, that each of us was soon engaged in earnest personal prayer, pleading that He would *now* endow us with the power he had promised.

Now he could!

Amid the soft drone of one hundred and twenty prayers in unity with their God and each other, there came throughout the room a sound that obviously was not man-made.

It originated from outside the building, and as we were to discover, it was attracting public attention.

I soon realized it was the roar of a mighty wind one associates with a thunder storm, though with an intensity such as I had never before experienced.

The walls of the room were noticeably vibrating, and though the windows and doors were closed, the wind entered the room and exploded upon us with such velocity as to anticipate that we would all be killed.

We were terrified!

Suddenly the wind was supercharged with an exploding fission that separated from its main source into tongue-like particles of flame, coming to rest upon the head of each of us, and in the same instant permeated our whole being, head to foot, with a power hitherto never experienced.

Terror gave way to adulation as our tongues were loosed and we each spoke the praises of God in a language that we had neither known nor spoken before, individually assigned to us by the Holy Spirit.

Suddenly, led by Peter, we all bolted for the door, down the stairs, and into the street.

We were loosed from our fears and apprehensions! We were supercharged with new energy! We were filled with a new spirit of praise and witness. We unceremoniously ran through the streets toward the Temple, drawing an ever-expanding entourage of inquisitors with us, as they each heard us praising God in their own language and demanding of us what was the meaning of it all.

An overflow crowd was celebrating Pentecost at the temple site, and now their ranks were swelled beyond capacity, as men and women of at least sixteen different national origins and languages, joined the celebrants.

They were about to hear the first sermon of gospel love and forgiveness ever preached!

The once cowardly disciples now stood amid those who sought their arrest and probable execution and fearlessly proclaimed Jesus of Nazareth to be the long-promised Messiah! The Son of God! The Savior of mankind!

He, who had denied his Lord three times in public, now stood before an immense crowd of his countrymen and began to speak!

The contents of that first Christian sermon are to be found in the second chapter of Acts of the Apostles, in the New Testament of the Christian Bible.

I address its results!

Horrified and repentant, the congregation, tearful to the point of wailing, knelt in the temple and in the streets of Jerusalem and begged the mercy and forgiveness of God for their sins.

The Christian Church began its ministry with the conversion of three thousand souls in a single day!

He had come with the wind!

Epilogue

My dear reader, I feel that an appropriate conclusion to this novel requires these additional comments to you personally.

Uppermost, is of course, my gratitude to you for taking the time to read my book. Without you the writing of it would have been superfluous.

My main concern has been, the coming to faith in Jesus Christ as Savior and Lord, and the strengthening of that faith, in all who should read it.

It is not for me to know whether, in addressing you personally, I write to a follower of Jesus; some hard-pressed struggling Christian; or to one who has little or no knowledge of the gospel of salvation.

Notwithstanding, I have prayed throughout its writing that this book would bring fresh focus to the love of God expressed in the life, death and resurrection of our Lord Jesus Christ, through the experiences of our real-life-hero, Nicodemus.

I am quite aware that my obligation to you does not conclude with your reading of this book.

It may well be that you have further concerns that you feel you must share with me: a personal testimony; perhaps a concern for your own personal salvation; or the need of further direction in your spiritual journey.

And yes, you may well need to vent your disagreement or criticism of what I have written.

May I invite you to have a personal dialogue with me through the marvel of the Internet? My email address is <u>dgoodridge@ shaw.ca</u>

Or, should you prefer to write me, the address is:
Don Goodridge
1832 Lipsett Court
Kelowna BC V1V 1X3
Canada

Now to conclude, may I ask that you read the concluding pages of the book, entitled "My Testimony?" I pray it may be of further assistance to you.

Oh yes! Before I forget; If you have found the book to be a good read, you might be willing to recommend it to your friends and acquaintances.

Thank you! God bless you!

My Confession!

A Personal Witness

As we come to the conclusion of this book I find myself compelled to bear witness to the truths presented here.

The immense spiritual implications of the Gospel of John, particularly in the third chapter, present enormous hope for both the unbeliever and the Christian. But I can also understand if it leaves a deep sense of spiritual inadequacy within one's soul.

"Is this for real?" "Is all this wishful thinking?" "Can it really happen?" "Has it really happened to anybody?"

These are legitimate questions and do not reflect any degree of spiritual inadequacy on the part of the enquirer.

To the contrary, they signify the stirring of the Holy Spirit in the life of the one who asks them.

If anyone even hinted that they had arrived at the pinnacle of all that God is and has and gives to his children, they would be proven false. Certainly, it can be said that all sincere seekers after God are *full* of his fullness to the degree of their current spiritual status.

The unbeliever finds himself/herself strangely moved in mind, heart and conscience. That is the Holy Spirit beginning the work of grace. The believer, confused, or discouraged, and spiritually hungry for more of that grace is ready to be filled with more of God. The most mature saint, irrespective of the immensity of their spiritual example, cries out to God for more, and more, and more! Even he who prayed this prayer for the family of God confessed concerning his current spiritual status:

"Not that I have already obtained all this, or have already been made perfect, but I press on to take hold of that for which Christ Jesus took hold of me. Brothers, I do not consider myself yet to have taken hold of it. But one thing I do: Forgetting what is behind and straining toward what is ahead, I press on toward the goal to win the prize for which God has called me heavenward in Christ Jesus. All of us who are mature should take such a view of things. And if on some point you think differently, that too God will make clear to you. Only let us live up to what we have already attained." (Philippians 3: 12 – 16;)

Please excuse the use of the first person singular in this chapter. I think it will be easier for you to relate to my experience since I am personally witnessing to *you* the reader.

In sharing with you, I emphatically give total glory, praise and thanksgiving to almighty God, who has done a great work in my life, beyond my deserving.

Nor would I deter you with any thought that my experience is something special or spectacular beyond the witness of countless others, whose experiences by far exceed my own.

I was fortunate to be born into a Christian home of loving and caring parents of humble means, the second of twin boys.

All my childhood and youth was spent within the fellowship of the Church. Those informative days were increasingly filled with the awareness of the need for a life of holiness, encouraged by the teachings of The Salvation Army.

From my earliest recollections, my mother told me that one day I would be a minister of the Gospel. Never, throughout those informative years, was there any coercion on her part, but within my childish breast there was planted a deep desire to become a Christian minister, of course as a Salvation Army officer (clergy).

In fact, as manhood approached, I found myself so intensely desirous of full time ministry that I was afraid God would not call me.

I "gave my heart to Jesus" at the age of seven, but I truly date my conversion at the age of thirteen, when at a revival meeting I gave myself to Christ under a conscious conviction of the Holy Spirit, and gave evidence to this experience by responding with a public prayer in that meeting with biblical truths far beyond my personal understanding at that time. This in turn led to my witnessing before many hundreds of people in a Salvation Army "Holiness Meeting."

Such an experience of course placed high expectations upon me within my denomination, since it seemed to them that I had attained spirituality beyond the expectations of my years.

None could tell, not even me, the spiritual struggles I would have throughout my youth and adult life in pursuit of the holy life; the agony of soul that I would experience in my search for, as Salvationists explain it, "the blessing of a clean heart."

But praise be to God, his hand was upon me. His plan was being fulfilled for my life without my awareness. The day would finally come when the ecstasy of my soul would know no bounds. In the meantime there was much work to be accomplished by the Holy Spirit.

The call to ministry really and truly came during a morning service at my local church, and shortly thereafter I entered training for my life's work.

I am still amazed to this day how God reaches out and plucks, despite the availability of more choice servants, such humble, unrefined and spiritually inept followers to lead his flock. But the wife of our minister, his co-pastor, gave me advice in two sentences that have proven their worth over forty-two years of full-time ministry and more than fourteen years of continued service in retirement. She said, "Don, there will be times when the Holy Spirit moves so rapidly, he will sweep you off your feet. But there will be other times when he moves so slowly that you will think that you have lost him." I was not to know that it would take the Holy Spirit twenty-two more years to bring me truly to my knees in complete surrender to his will, at the very brink of spiritual disaster.

How excited I was, and not a little proud, that at last I was launched on my career. I was well received in all of my various appointments. I truly reveled in the ministry and never lost the deep conviction of my calling. I could do nothing else with my life. Time and time again this conviction saved me from the lure of more lucrative "secular" work when the economic depression of my profession would test my faith.

In fact, I was filled with pride at my own survival in the ministry, and I allowed myself an overt ambition as to the heights I would attain as I rose up the ladder of success. All the while, the struggle continued in the deep recesses of my soul with an agonizing hunger for "something more" in my spiritual experience.

I continuously floundered in my search for a life of holiness. Again and again I would succumb to bitter disappointment, as sin would overcome me despite my strongest determination to do better.

I would not have you think that my ministry was void of blessing and some "successes" as some might count them. Souls were saved, people were blessed, and I generally enjoyed the accolades of my colleagues and my superiors. But to my mind I was a hypocrite because I had created a "spiritual front" that masked the agony of my own soul.

In his infinite love, God shifted my focus from my personal efforts to obtain holiness of life, to the person of the Holy Spirit and began to teach me that holiness of heart is not self-achieved but can only be realized by the total surrender of my will, body and mind and spirit, to the indwelling Holy Spirit.

Still the struggle continued. My focus was more on what others expected of me than what God desired for me. This inevitably coerced me into doing everything in my own strength. I was excessively focused on what people thought of me and not on how much God loved me. In fact, although I truly believed he did, I was unable to assimilate that love into my spirit because I had no respect for myself.

You can only imagine the burden I placed on my family as I unwittingly made my expectations theirs, and expected discipline and conformity that would serve the purpose of masking the misery of own my soul.

I have no doubt I truly loved my dear wife and our five children. But I was unable to express that love in the unconditional terms wherewith God loves us all, because I had placed conditions on my concept of his love by my persistence in judging myself.

Inevitably Satan closed in for the kill!

In reality, without my comprehension, God in his infinite wisdom was permitting me to come to the end of myself.

Defeated on every front, my personal life, my ministry and my family life, all came crashing down around me. I found myself in total despair to the point I actually prayed that God would take my life. I just wanted to get it over with.

Of great significance was seemingly the loss of my Christian faith. It was all over! It just didn't work! It was all a lie! At least I thought it was. I had nothing more to give. I no longer believed that God, or whoever or whatever, could have anything more to do with me. I had come to the absolute end of self, and, in retrospect, imagined I could hear God say to the angels "At last! It's about time!"

The next day, being Sunday, I found myself for the first time in my Christian adult life not wanting to go to church.

But what would people say? My wife didn't drive. There was no bus service. The kids needed to get to Sunday school and it would most certainly be that members of the congregation would see me drop the family off and make a hasty retreat.

No! I was not the pastor of the church at the time. I was engaged in special work for my denomination and was now a member of the congregation. But about half the congregation had been our flock some years earlier, which in my opinion didn't help the present situation one bit.

Pride, and fear of what people would say took over and I went into the Bible class like nothing had ever happened. During the leader's presentation, the Holy Spirit fell upon that group and a dear lady began to weep aloud. She said, "You people have got something I haven't got and I want it." Of all the bombastic hypocritical gall of a guy that had "just lost his faith," I heard myself say spontaneously "Helen (not her real name) you need Jesus Christ as your Savior." If the angels in Heaven had sent an immediate delegation of protest to the Heavenly Father at that point, I would fully understand it. But God wasn't through with me yet, no more than He is now!

The class closed down at that point so one of the women could take that dear seeking soul to a counseling room to lead her to Christ. While that was going on God was setting me up!

During the singing of the opening hymn in the morning worship service that followed, God called me to kneel at the altar of prayer, in the front of the church, it seemed with a mighty shout from the rear of the sanctuary that all could hear. I protested in my heart that such a move would completely disturb the service. But God wasn't listening! He called again, and at the point of promising if he would call me at the traditional invitation time at the end of the service, I would respond, he lost all patience.

To this day I cannot remember any physical move on my part, other than I found myself being propelled toward the mercy seat, whereupon God began a reconstruction job in my soul, and the souls of many others who joined me at the altar that morning, in a great outpouring of the Holy Spirit upon that congregation.

God required much of me during that long session upon my knees. He demanded absolute surrender of every aspect of my life and those intimately associated with it.

Starting with my wife, and each of my children in turn, he demanded ownership of each of them and my confession that I had messed things up in my relationships with them.

He turned to my career, and read the riot act upon my pride, my overt ambition, my legalistic attitude and my lack of love for

God's children. He demanded ownership of it all. But He wasn't finished!

He turned upon my sin, my sinning, my sinfulness, and demanded that I confess it all and admit that I had no control over any of it. If he didn't help me now, nothing would. But he wasn't finished!

Now he demanded a fresh surrender of my total person, body, mind and spirit to his supreme control. It was immediately apparent that there was to be nothing held back. He wasn't interested in my theology. He didn't care about my position in the body of Christ. He was unimpressed with any and all accomplishments, real or imagined, and it was emphatically true if he did not get such an unconditional surrender of my life, here and now, there was no further blessing available by reason of my own rebellion.

But his timing was perfect. There was nothing left of "Me." And when I had nothing else left to offer him; nothing held back, he sent me on my way with the aching void of an emptied soul clean scrubbed by his Spirit of forgiveness. But he wasn't finished!

That evening, at home, my wife and I spoke a long time about the crisis that had befallen us, and I was able to profusely apologize for my past attitude and mistakes, for which there was her instant and full forgiveness. But there still remained the aching void of a soul that needed to be filled, with what, I did not know. But God wasn't finished!

The next morning I went to the office early, as was my custom, to have my private devotions before the staff arrived. I sat in my chair before God and began to pray, "Father God, this is day one in a *new relationship* with you. I'm like a little child afraid to take my first step. I don't know what comes next, but I cannot go anywhere or do anything this day without your help."

"Lord, I have heard that a person can be baptized in the Spirit, and I confess that I haven't a clue what that means, whether the trumpets will blare, the thunder roar and the lightning flash. But

Lord you know that I cannot go on without such a blessing, and I am not going to lift up the pen off this desk until you baptize me with your Holy Spirit."

In that very instant I received the baptism of the Holy Spirit!

There was no waiting, save that out of my desperation I should ask. There was not a sound, nothing demonstrative, but simultaneously that office room and the void of my soul were filled with the overwhelming presence of God. The Spirit had come! How did I know? In the immediate moments that followed I was filled with the unconditional *love* of God. That whole room became a Holy of Holies for this self-impoverished soul.

The Holy Spirit filled me with wave after wave of agapé love; Holy Spirit love; God's love, with such intensity that my torso was pressed into the very desk top, and currents of divine power surged through me from the top of my head to the soles of my feet, like electric charges. So overwhelming was the experience that I finally had to beg the Lord to stay His hand for fear He would kill me with the very blessing that would lead me into a new and wonderful life in the Spirit.

The superlatives with which I have described the blessing are not to be misconstrued as being essentially or solely indicative of the same blessing afforded to others. Never did I then or now consider such emotional and physical signs of His coming to be the essence of the baptism.

There are three all-important facts of witness that sum up the experience. Firstly, not only was I filled with the divine love of God to be poured out of me to others, at last I was able to love myself. The guilt was gone. Self was under the Spirit's control. I was really and truly a new creature in Christ Jesus to the extent I had never known before.

Secondly, the Holy Spirit spoke directly to my consciousness and said, "You will never judge another individual again." I sincerely pray that you know of the incredible spiritual liberty that such an edict brings to the believer.

Thirdly, I was enabled to witness to the mercy and goodness of God and to make confession of my sins against others, to seek their forgiveness, starting that very morning with each member of my staff, my beloved pastors, my wife and my children, all of whom are forgiven for their skepticism at such a dramatic change they now observed in one I am sure they had merely tolerated.

A new and exciting ministry opened to me as, over a number of years, my ministry responsibilities sent me into the guest pulpits of over seventy-five churches within my denomination and a number of others, where I was able to witness to the faithfulness of God to the infilling of his Holy Spirit.

Many were led into the blessing through those meetings and thirty-four plus years later I never tire of telling my story.

Finally, after twenty-two years of ministry, at the age of forty-two, I had been baptized with the Holy Spirit. What now? Well, time and space deny me the opportunity to share with you the joy in my service to Christ in these subsequent years. Please be patient with me. God is, and He isn't finished with me yet!